Marta Oulie

Marta Oulie

A Novel of Betrayal

SIGRID UNDSET

Introduction by Jane Smiley

Translated by Tiina Nunnally

University of Minnesota Press
Minneapolis

The translator thanks the National Endowment for the Arts for a 2004 NEA Translation Fellowship, which made this translation possible, and Nan Bentzen Skille, who read the translation in manuscript and offered helpful suggestions.

Originally published as *Fru Marta Oulie* by H. Aschehoug & Co. in Kristiania (Oslo), Norway, in 1907

Introduction copyright 2014 by Jane Smiley

English translation copyright 2014 by Tiina Nunnally

Published by the University of Minnesota Press
111 Third Avenue South, Suite 290
Minneapolis, MN 55401-2520
http://www.upress.umn.edu

LIBRARY OF CONGRESS CATALOGING-IN-PUBLICATION DATA
Undset, Sigrid, 1882–1949. [Fru Marta Oulie. English]
Marta Oulie: a novel of betrayal / Sigrid Undset; Introduction by Jane Smiley; Translated by Tiina Nunnally.
ISBN 978-0-8166-9252-1 (pb)
1. Europe—History—Fiction. I. Nunnally, Tiina, 1952– translator. II. Title.
PT8950.U5F713 2014
839.823'72—dc23   2013046280

Printed in the United States of America on acid-free paper

The University of Minnesota is an equal-opportunity educator and employer.

20 19 18 17 16 15 14   10 9 8 7 6 5 4 3 2 1

CONTENTS

INTRODUCTION

Jane Smiley

When she began her debut novella, *Fru Marta Oulie,* in the summer of 1906, Sigrid Undset had just turned twenty-four. She had submitted a previous historical work to a prominent publisher in Denmark and been rejected, so she took up a subject that was very current: how women are to arrange their lives, how they should think of themselves, and how their inner lives, both intellectual and emotional, should fit into their existence. Marta Oulie is a married woman in her thirties with four children who has been unfaithful to her husband with her cousin. She narrates her story as a series of first-person diary entries. Sigrid Undset was an unmarried woman in her early twenties who had no children. Her first book cannot have been based on personal experience, but she embraced this subject and poured so much effort and feeling into it that twenty years later, when she was considered for the Nobel Prize in Literature, the committee "focused on her debut novel . . . and on *Kristin Lavransdatter*, praising the author for her extraordinary power and originality, both in her examination of the human soul and as a storyteller."[1] Undset was not an autobiographical writer but a speculative, inquisitive one; her genius was empathy, the ability to enter into the mind of someone unlike herself (male or female, modern or medieval) and to body forth the feelings and the perceptions of that character, thereby reaffirming that human beings can and should understand each other across the barriers of time, geography, age, and gender.

But Marta was not born in a vacuum. During the first years of the twentieth century, the proper role of women was under discussion in the city of Kristiania (later Oslo). Feminist ideas were popular, and they included issues of sexuality and reproduction. The debate could be acrimonious. Henrik Ibsen's play *A Doll's House*, though twenty-one years old at the turn of the century, was well on its way to becoming the most frequently produced play of the twentieth century. Writers such as Gunnar Heiberg ["Balkonen" ("The Balcony," 1894) and "Kjærlighedens tragedie" ("Love's Tragedy," 1904)] and Hulda Garborg [*Kvinden skabt af manden* (*Woman Created by Man*, 1904) and *Fru Evas dagbog* (*Mrs. Eva's Diary*, 1905)] initiated the debate, but they

1. Nan Bentzen Skille, *Inside the Gate: Sigrid Undset's Life at Bjerkebæk*, trans. Tiina Nunnally (Oslo: H. Aschehoug & Co., 2009), 174.

were a generation older than Undset. Theater, newspapers, and literature were all afire, and Marta waded in with her bold first sentence: "I have been unfaithful to my husband." Readers in the twenty-first century, inured to movies, plays, and fiction about infidelity, and for whom divorce is a routine social issue (even if a personal crisis), may be more shocked by Marta's other experiences—the death of her husband, apparently the icon of strength and beauty, from tuberculosis within months (and no one even imagines a cure); her affair with her own first cousin; her isolation with no one to confide in and nowhere to turn when her story is finished. But Marta's voice retains its power and intimacy, and we experience her uncertainty and despair step by step as events unfold and she reviews her life. Undset's ability to evoke the immediacy of Marta's emotions, and the settings in which they play themselves out, is one of her signal talents, one that would blossom in her mature works, the books she wrote after she encountered romantic passion, marital disappointment, and maternal difficulties.

Sigrid Undset was born in Denmark in May 1882, the daughter of archaeologist Ingvald Undset and his Danish wife, Anna Maria Charlotte Gyth. Ingvald Undset was a successful and productive scholar who specialized in the study of Iron Age Europe. He worked at the Museum of National Antiquities in Kristiania and received a stipend for his work from the Norwegian government. After falling ill on a trip to Rome in 1882, he died at the age of forty when Sigrid was eleven, leaving a wife and three daughters.

Undset took a secretarial course and went to work at the age of sixteen, but she was ambitious and curious; while holding her first job, she worked on a historical novel, set in the Middle Ages, undoubtedly inspired by her father's studies and exploring classic themes of Norse literature, including rape, revenge, and pride.

Her next book (and the first published), *Fru Marta Oulie,* achieved the best kind of success for a young writer: upon publication, it made money and generated controversy. Undset was praised for her protagonist's up-to-date, natural, and conversational voice and for her talent in exploring her characters' idiosyncrasies. Some critics found Marta too modern and too self-involved; others thought her honesty made her sympathetic. The effect on Undset was inspirational: she wrote a friend that she was full of ideas for more books and pleased with her earnings (600 kroner). She published ten books in the next twelve years, including *Fortællingen om Viga-Ljot og Vigdis* (*Gunnar's Daughter,* 1909). *Jenny* (1911) and *Vaaren* (*Spring,* 1914) explored similar themes as *Fru Marta Oulie.* In 1920, at the age of thirty-eight, Undset published the first volume of what is considered her greatest work, *Kristin Lavransdatter,* set in fourteenth-century Norway—the work that earned her the Nobel Prize in 1928.

Literary and popular success enabled Sigrid Undset to shape her own life in a way that Marta cannot. In 1909, Undset went to Rome, where she met and fell in love with Norwegian artist Anders Castus Svarstad, who was thirteen years older than she was and already married, with three children. They married three years later, after his divorce, and lived for a while in Kristiania (though Anders spent time pursuing his artistic vocation in Rome and Paris). In 1919, the family was evicted from their apartment. Although they had contracted for another place to live, they could not, for practical reasons, move into it, and Undset, pregnant with her third child, took the train to Lillehammer, then something of an artist's colony. There she found her future home, an old-fashioned timbered house on a little more than an acre on the outskirts of town. She purchased the property one year later with profits from the first volume of *Kristin Lavransdatter, Kransen (The Wreath)*. For the next twenty years, Undset devoted her life to rearing her children, writing her books (seventeen volumes, including the second and third parts of *Kristin Lavransdatter* and another set, *Olav Audunssøn i Hestviken* and *Olav Audunssøn og hans børn*, which are usually published in English as a tetralogy, *The Master of Hestviken*).

Undset's marriage to Anders Svarstad was beset with difficulties that somewhat resembled those suffered by Marta Oulie. Svarstad proved neither faithful nor reliable as a husband. He did not care to live in Lillehammer, and for the most part he left the care of the children to Undset, a responsibility that was especially challenging because their daughter, Maren, had severe learning disabilities from birth. Even before her marriage was annulled in 1924, Undset was living Marta Oulie's life—supporting herself as a single mother with children. But in the two decades since writing *Marta Oulie,* Undset had answered the questions that she leaves unresolved at the end of her first novella.

Perhaps the most powerful section of *Marta Oulie* is after Otto's death. Marta has found marriage frustrating. Her husband, for whom she felt such early passion, has loved her faithfully but not understood her, or seemed to want to. Issues of taste, lifestyle, and intellect that compose Marta's sense of who she is mean nothing to him, and so she has the affair with Henrik. After Otto dies (never knowing of the affair), Henrik tells Marta that perhaps he has a prior claim to her love, since he has loved her his entire life; he feels her marriage to Otto was her seminal betrayal. Henrik would like to marry her, support her, re-create the family life with her that she has lost. Marta, wracked with guilt, cannot allow such a thing, and it is clear at the end that she does not know how to proceed. The final image in *Marta Oulie* is an injured child staring obsessively at her injury. The ending is evocative but indicates the limits of Undset's twenty-four-year-old imagination. In 1924, at the age of forty-two, Sigrid Undset did understand how to move forward. Not only did she keep writing and developing her property (especially her gardens), she also converted (scandalously for her time and place) to Catholicism. For the next twenty-five years, she was actively involved in the church, and she was sincere and industrious about constructing her life according to the precepts of faith and good works; when she received the Nobel Prize, for example, she donated the financial award to three charitable foundations. Her conversion (from agnosticism, although she was a Lutheran; we may read Marta's lack of faith as resembling that of her creator) caused considerable scandal in Norway, since Lutheranism was the state religion. There was no Catholic church in Lillehammer, so Undset used a building she had brought to her property for services. Her conversion seemed animated by, and did further animate, her literary work.

An author's life and his or her writing are always in dialogue with one another, especially when the author is, like Sigrid Undset, inquisitive, speculative, ready to do research. An author writes a novel, but the novel may indeed convince the author of something that he or she was wondering about when the subject presented itself. After writing *David Copperfield*, for example, Charles Dickens decided that his marriage was over and constructed a wall between his room and his wife's, then left her. The idea of *Marta Oulie* spoke to the young Sigrid Undset perhaps at first because of her father's death and her own adolescence as the daughter of a single mother, for whom the issues of female identity were of primary importance. She could explore this topic, but she could not solve the problem, though she returned to it over and over. In the end, her definition of female identity—at least regarding her own—was based on hard work, faith, and charity. *Marta Oulie* is an unusually sophisticated and frank book for a young writer—shocking in its day, prophetic in hindsight, and well worth reading.

Marta Oulie

Part 1

I have been unfaithful to my husband.

I write that down and sit and stare at the words, which fill my thoughts. The same way I once wrote Otto's name and stared at it: *Otto Oulie, Otto Oulie, Otto Oulie.*

March 26, 1902

Otto's letters arrive as precisely as Thursday and Saturday arrive. He's in good spirits and writes that things are progressing well. After I read them, I'm always left with the same feeling of disappointment. They're so impersonal, even though he almost always writes about the children and our home, and then a little about life up there in the sanitarium. But he might as well be talking about some other home and other children.

I'm ashamed of myself for thinking about things like that—I focus my attention on his businesslike penmanship and businesslike tone. Yet from every single letter I can sense that he is longing for all of us, my poor boy, and that he loves us.

Incidentally, I can't seem to put together a single natural-sounding or unrestrained letter. I write only about the children, but I can see how badly my letters are written. Otto probably doesn't notice.

April 2, 1902

Otto's letter today was more melancholy than any of the previous ones. He is longing terribly for home. He says that he spent all afternoon reading through the old letters from me and the boys, looking at our photographs. "I kiss the pictures of all of you every single evening. The little photo that Henrik took of you and Einar at the cabin hangs over my bed, but I take it down and kiss it every evening just before I turn off the light."

He says that I must come to visit him at Easter. Yes, my dear, I will certainly come. Oh, I do long for you, too, Otto. But what I long for is the impossible. It's something that I would give my life and my soul to have undone. Oh, to have a free, healthy, clear conscience! Then nothing could steal my courage away from me—no, you would gain strength and hope and vitality with every word I wrote or spoke to you. I would be both father and mother to the children while you were away.

Then I wouldn't have a single thought for myself, only for my dear ones and for you, Otto, wishing that you would regain your health. I feel so wretched about the fact that I'm always going around brooding and thinking about my own problems. But I can't let them go even for an instant. And the situation is as bad today as when it was fresh, or perhaps even worse, because I have to bear it all alone, lock it inside so it lies like a cancerous wound on my spirit. And I'm reminded of it twenty times a day. I find it unbearable when Otto writes to ask whether I've seen anything of Henrik recently, whether he often comes to see us, and the like. He talks about him in almost every single letter. And then all those greetings to Åse: "my little Sweetheart that Father has hardly seen." He always wants to hear everything about her.

God knows what would happen if one day I told Otto: "Åse is not your child. Henrik and I, the two of us, about whom you have believed the best in the world and loved the most, we have betrayed you. Henrik is Åse's father."

I don't know what he would do. I can't even imagine. I know only that his life would be destroyed so thoroughly that nothing would be left of it. Where would he turn with such a boundless, appalling grievance? The fact that we betrayed him, while he himself was so faithful, painfully faithful in every way. Ever since we were married, I've seen how he lives for his home, for me and the children—as if we were his creditors, and it was our right to take every hour that he could spare and every øre he earned.

I don't think he even really believes that anything of that sort—infidelity and adultery—could happen to him. On the periphery of his life a man might occasionally "seduce a woman" or betray his wife, or marry a "slut," but Otto's view of things is terribly uncomplicated. About such cases he would always say that he or she ought to be shot or stuffed into a sack and tossed into the Aker River.

Poor Otto. And poor me.

April 3, 1902

I've begun keeping a diary again. I also kept a diary when I fell in love with Otto, but back then I didn't manage to write much. At the time I didn't feel like sitting down and thinking about myself.

In the past I was always shocked when I read books that claimed a woman could be happy only if she devoted herself completely to another person. Now I say yes and amen to that, as I do to all the other hackneyed and worn-down truths that I rebelled against in my youth.

Now I understand why a criminal confesses, and why Catholic women become addicted to confession.

I once said that I would be capable of committing a murder and continuing to live with my own conscience as confidante and judge to punish or pardon me. Good Lord, now I go around thinking about confessing to someone. I lie awake and ponder such matters all through the night. For instance, what if one of the children, as an adult, should someday end up in great mental anguish and confess to his mother—would I then tell the young person everything, to frighten and warn and strengthen and help and save him? How awful.

It would be so refreshing to sit in a confessional and

spill out everything to a priest behind a grating and then go home, relieved and cleansed, with a clear conscience. Or to be able to serve my sentence in jail. Instead, I'm sitting here now, writing page after page. And good Lord, what a miserable wretch I've become! I had imagined that I would think less about it in the daytime and lie awake less often at night. To some extent, that's true, but it's more likely because I've had the Easter cleaning to tend to.

Tomorrow I leave for Lillehammer.

June 22, 1902

I'm trying to write again because I can no longer tolerate my own thoughts. It feels as if some superhuman imagination had thought everything out and made the situation as unbearable and painful and upsetting as possible. I'm almost at the point of being converted to believe in Providence again.

I've betrayed my husband—who is young and handsome and kind and faithful and noble and dear—with his best friend Henrik, who is his partner and my cousin. I've known Henrik since we were children, and he was the one who brought me and Otto together. And now Otto is lying up there at Grefsen with consumption, and my lover is paying his expenses and supporting all the rest of us. And Otto hasn't a clue in the world. I can't go and visit him without hearing him talk about what an excellent friend Henrik is, and what an excellent wife he has. When all is said and done, it seems the child we've foisted on him is dearest to his heart. She's the one he always asks about.

I found out about the whole wretched business when I went to visit Otto during Easter week. He wanted to come home, but when I said that I thought he had better stay there until he was well, he replied that he couldn't keep on accepting financial support from Henrik. When Otto first went there, he thought he would be well in a couple of months, at least well enough to be able to start back at the office. Then I learned that when Otto and Henrik started the company, Henrik invested all his capital in Otto's fledgling business. I had always thought that Otto had inherited *something* from his father, even though it might not have been much. But it turned out there was nothing. The business did well, and he had good connections, but there was too little money to work with. Even though Otto is a very clever businessman, he says that Henrik acted as a good friend back then.

"I worked like a horse as long as I had my health," said Otto. "And I had no qualms about leaving when Henrik suggested it, but I can't just stay here for years in practically the most expensive health resort in the whole country."

I almost told him everything. It was so horrible the minute I heard that. I could only agree with Otto. I suggested that we could rent a place outside the city, and I would take such good care of him, such good care . . . Dear God, how I begged him. It was also because I wanted so much to do something for him, and Otto was very touched. He wept with his head on my shoulder and kept patting my cheek and hands. But he refused, for the sake of the children. The poor man. I realized that he didn't dare attempt to live with us under such straitened circumstances. It's terrible to see how he suffers and clings to life. He's frightened.

He came back with me and was home for three weeks. I was happy to have him here, because I can hardly bear to be alone anymore. But my God, how dreadful it was, all the same. And to see how scared he was that he might infect the children, and yet they clung to him, as he did to them.

He went to the office every day, and I constantly had to hear about Henrik. Otto often brought him home for both the midday meal and supper. It wasn't any better for Henrik, and that gave me some comfort. How pathetic I've become. In silence I would look to see if Henrik had gotten more gray in his hair during the past couple of years, but no matter how hard I looked, I couldn't see that he has changed at all since he came back from England.

Otto is back at Grefsen now. He started spitting up great quantities of blood right after he returned and is still in bed.

I've taken a teaching position at my old school, starting after the holidays. Of course I'm overjoyed about it. The children and I will be able to live with almost no financial help from the business. On the other hand, I've grown so lazy from living as well as I have over the past few years. At heart I suppose I'd prefer to sit in an armchair and brood all day long. I dread having to pull myself together and start working again.

On the afternoon when it was decided that Otto should go to Grefsen, Henrik came to see me in the children's room where I was sitting.

"As long as Otto is ill, we must try to pretend that there was never anything between us, Marta," he said. "We must!"

He's right, and he ought to be hanged—as the saying goes.

June 25, 1902

Tomorrow is Åse's first birthday. This has been the longest year of my life. I feel so guilty about my little girl. I don't think I've been a good enough mother for her, or for the other three either—no doubt our home is far from what it ought to be.

Oh, my sweet children. I really must pull myself together. You should see only smiles and sunshine and hear kind words spoken at home. But lately things have already begun to go downhill. And not only because the boys are getting bigger and don't come to me to be cuddled like they used to do. When I gather all three of the older children around me in the afternoon, they no longer lay their heads on my lap or snuggle close; they no longer compete for their mother's attention.

I'm dreading tomorrow. I can't very well cheat the children out of the traditional birthday party with hot chocolate. Einar and Halfred came to me, asking for help in wriggling some coins out of their piggy banks. They wanted to buy presents for their baby sister. I had to force myself to be patient, and of course they noticed that. They crept away, looking so crestfallen. Poor little things . . .

I also have to go visit Otto tomorrow.

July 3, 1902

Today is my wedding anniversary.

I took the three older children with me to visit him. I simply didn't dare go there alone. I noticed that Otto wasn't really pleased that I had brought them along. It was pouring rain, and that was also one reason why they shouldn't have come, according to Otto. "They're warmly dressed, aren't they, dear? Let me feel your legs, children—you're not cold, are you? What about you, Marta? Oh, my dear, I'm sure that you're careful. I suppose you know how necessary it is. For God's sake, take care that they don't catch cold."

He was up and sitting in an armchair. I almost cried every time I looked at him. How pitifully thin he has become, and his clothes are much too big for him. He tried to converse with me and the children, but it wasn't really successful. Einar and Halfred and Ingrid sat on their chairs, hanging their heads. We had to have a glass of wine, and after I clinked glasses with Otto, he took both of my hands in his and kissed them quietly. "Thank you, my Marta," was all he said. That was too much for me. I burst into tears, and

Ingrid promptly started crying. She ran over and hid her face in my lap. I had to take her in my arms and comfort her. When I glanced over at Otto again, he was leaning back in his chair with his eyes closed. His lips were quivering.

Fortunately the weather cleared and the children could be sent to the park. From the window we could see the three small figures moving along the lane of birches.

"It's a pity to bring them with you, Marta," said Otto. "It's no fun for them to come here."

I didn't reply.

"I said it's no fun for them to come here," he repeated, annoyed.

That's almost the saddest thing of all, that peevish, tormented tone of voice that he sometimes uses. He never talked like that before he fell ill.

"If only we'd had some inkling about this eleven years ago, you and I," he said quietly. "I wish we had. Then you wouldn't be sitting here with four young children and a wreck of a husband. How different everything looked back then, Marta. This wasn't what we were expecting . . . Do you remember," he said as he squeezed my hands so hard that it hurt, "it was eleven years ago today . . . and how marvelous you have been all this time. Marta, my own dear heart. I wonder if you know how much I love you? I thank you for all these years . . ."

IT STARTED RAINING AGAIN, and the children came back upstairs. It was so late that the doctor appeared, making his evening rounds. As we were about to leave, Otto drew the children close.

"I suppose you're all behaving nicely and obeying your mother while Father is away? You're being very sweet, aren't you? You must never, ever cause your mother any trouble, children. Do you hear me, Einar? You're big enough to remember what Father tells you. You must always be a good, well-mannered boy, always do whatever you can for your mother and your brother and sisters. You too, Halfred, my boy."

They cried and I cried. We were a sorry procession as we walked back down the road under our umbrellas to the tram. And then Ingrid wet herself and I had to pick her up and carry her, otherwise we would never have reached town. I had my hands full, holding the child and the umbrella, the hem of my skirts wet and both boys trudging behind me on that abysmal road in the pouring rain.

A year ago today I was recovering from the birth of my little girl. Otto sat beside me and comforted me—we might still be a happy couple on our golden wedding anniversary. He couldn't honestly have imagined for even an instant that he was not going to regain his health.

Two years ago we were staying at the cabin, as we always did on our wedding anniversary. We toasted each other and drank champagne, and Otto said that he thought he was the happiest man in Norway. I sat there thinking about how boundlessly unhappy I was—how estranged we had become from one another—back then he had no idea. I didn't know what real unhappiness could be!

By next year I may be a widow.

We've put the cabin up for sale. I can only hope it won't sell too quickly in these hard times—at least not while Otto is still alive.

WHEN I THINK ABOUT OUR MARRIAGE, what happened seems somehow inevitable. But it also still seems so senseless—and stupid. All my sorrows run together into anger and bitterness, and I can't direct them toward anyone but myself. In reality, a person doesn't have much choice about what to do in this world. If I had known back then, when Otto and I began to slip away from each other, what I know now . . . oh, we could have been happy today! Yet if I could live the past five or six years over again, and be the same person I was then, I know that it would have all turned out the same way.

THE FIRST TIME I SAW OTTO was on September 2. I was walking along Kirkegaden in glorious sunshine, wearing my black silk dress and tasseled cap. I was going to celebrate the fourth anniversary of my graduation from secondary school with several others from the group. I ran into Henrik, and he walked along with me. At the bottom of the hill a gentleman hurried past at great speed, shouting hello. Fiery red hair, lots of freckles, superb physique—that was my impression. I asked who he was.

"Oh, that's Oulie," says Henrik. "He works at the offices of Berg and Bache. Wood pulp, you know."

"What a handsome way he has of walking," I said, turning around. The gentleman had stopped farther up the street and was looking back at us.

"He's awfully pleasant, a decent sort of fellow," said Henrik.

A couple of days later Henrik said, "I bring you greetings from Oulie. It looks as though you made a deep impression on him."

Two days later I was invited to coffee and punch at Henrik's lodgings. The first thing I saw when I came in was Otto's red hair. The guests included the two of us and one other woman.

I was twenty-two back then, and I had never been in love. I had worked hard and been very diligent. People thought I was a cold fish. It was true that I was quiet and reserved. But really it was because I was shy.

As for Otto, I instantly felt superior to him. This was because I noticed at once, as Henrik said, that I had made a deep impression on Oulie. I also soon understood that he was the one who had asked Henrik to introduce him to me. When I thanked him for sending me his greetings, he turned bright red. "It didn't make you mad?" he asked several times. "You see, I knew who you were. People say that you're terribly clever. After all, you received the highest marks for both your diploma and teaching degree."

He escorted me home that evening. After I went to bed, I discovered that I could remember in overwhelmingly sharp detail every little thing about Otto Oulie's appearance. A thin, bony face, red hair, big, light-brown eyes, and lots of dark freckles; lips that were very delicate and beautifully shaped; and magnificent teeth, the two upper ones in front overlapping ever so slightly. I remember how clearly I could see his lips in my mind. I had noticed his physique the minute I saw him. In reality, I've never seen a man with so handsome a figure as Otto: slender and strong and elegant. There was something so exquisite about him and the way he carried himself. He made you think of a fine pedigreed animal, a truly delightful dog.

He looked younger than he was, because he turned twenty-six a couple of months later. But on that evening at Henrik's, with his smooth-shaven face and turned-down collar and blue suit, I didn't think he was more than twenty-two or three.

The next day I ran into him as I left school. After that we met daily. At first it seemed coincidental; then we agreed to meet. I told myself: "Why shouldn't I be allowed to meet a friend?"

One afternoon we went for a walk and a fierce rainstorm blew in. We happened to be on the street where he lived. "Would it be permissible for me to invite you up to my lodgings for a while?" he asked, looking embarrassed. "I have quite a nice room, by the way," he said as he opened the door.

In one corner stood a tall iron bedstead and a washstand made of tin. Against one wall, beneath a painting, stood a plush sofa with a table and two armchairs, just like in a pastry shop. There was also a mirror with a potted plant on a shelf underneath it in the corner, and he had a piano. He was very proud of his lodgings. He conferred at length with his landlady out in the hallway, and then she came in with coffee and fresh baked pastries. She was wearing an apron trimmed with a Hardanger border and looked unspeakably respectable. Otto introduced me as Miss Benneche, graduate and teacher.

Otto was terribly formal as a host. My hand actually shook a bit as I served the coffee. Otto's hand did the same as he held a match to my cigarette. In the mirror I saw that my cheeks were a blazing red, and my hair was very curly. That was from the rain. I looked nice, and I could see that he thought so, too.

Afterward I persuaded him to sing. I knew that he was a member of the Professional Merchants Choir Association. "I don't really know much," he said as he sat at the piano. He sang "I Wonder What I'll See." He had a beautiful tenor voice and sang in a rather sentimental fashion.

The whole time I could feel a slight trembling inside, as if from excitement. I had an urge to walk around and touch the things that surrounded him every day. Even though we had said so little to each other, I felt as if we had grown quite close.

As I put on my hat in front of the mirror, I stole a leaf

from his plant and hid it inside my glove. Otto later put it in a little gold medallion for me, and we've celebrated that day ever since. When Otto helped me with my jacket I had a sudden desire to tip my head back and lean it against his hand. I knew that it was up to me what would happen next. And I felt an intense, miserly joy at holding back—nothing more would happen that day.

I was invited back for his birthday. There were several other guests, but I didn't even notice them. I sat on the folding chair by the window, and Otto pulled a footstool over and sat near me. He sat there all evening. I had his face right below me the whole time. I have no idea what we talked about; Otto doesn't either.

"Hey, come on, Oulie," Henrik shouted once. "What a charming host you are. We're drinking a toast to you!"

"My dear friend," said Otto and went over to the table. I sank back in my chair, exhausted, as if after a long period of strain. It didn't occur to me for an instant that I ought to go over and join in the toast.

A little later he came back and sat on the footstool. I had a feeling that the air between our faces was quivering, as if around a flame.

We agreed on a sledding expedition when we parted.

OTTO INSISTED ON PULLING ME on the sled up all the hills. I sat there, lost in a daze, staring at his shoulders. How strong he is, I thought, and suddenly felt a sensual pang ripple through me. I had actually spent the past few months in an uninterrupted, nerve-wracking state of excitement. But at that moment it was as if for the first time I became aware that I loved him. Emotion overwhelmed me, and I suddenly felt quite powerless. It was fear and shyness and pride and joy all at once.

There were plenty of people in the hearth room that evening; the air was thick with tobacco smoke and cooking smells, and everyone was talking at a deafening pitch. But it all seemed far away. Otto had sat down right across from me. He had unbuttoned his Nansen jacket. Underneath he was wearing a blue flannel shirt with a soft collar. He was hot and slightly out of breath. I suddenly felt scared and didn't dare look at the scrap of his chest visible below his throat, but then couldn't resist glancing at it. At that moment he looked at me, and we couldn't take our eyes off each other but didn't say a word.

"*Skål,* Marta," said one of the women.

"Oh, excuse me," I said, flustered and turning red.

As we left the hearth room, Otto said in a strangely husky voice—he hadn't spoken to me since we left the town behind—"Sit down and I'll pull you."

We reached Frogner Hill, and he sat behind me on the sled. As I leaned against him, I felt as if I were surrendering, utterly and completely.

We parted from the others at Sporveisgaden. "I'm going to escort Miss Benneche home," he said. We reached my front door, and I got up from the sled. I didn't have my key.

"Maybe mine will work," he mumbled. He unlocked the door.

"Good night!"

"Good night!" He stepped inside the door. Then he suddenly took me in his arms and kissed me. I had never kissed a man before. I felt as if I dissolved.

After I went upstairs, I sat for a long time on the edge of my bed, wearing my wet ski clothes. I sat there as if intoxicated, aware only of my own heart beating, strong and erratic, making me shake. God in Heaven, imagine that I should be allowed to feel this happy. I awoke when the clock in my landlady's room struck four. As I got undressed, the thought raced, hot and fearful, through me several times: What if he doesn't love me in that way? What if it's merely passion? These words and thoughts belonged to someone else. They appeared for a second but vanished again; they had no meaning for me. I sank into my joyous intoxication.

The next morning, when I came out to the street with my schoolbooks under my arm, Otto Oulie was standing on the corner. He looked deep into my eyes, took the essay books, and said: "To think that you're willing to be my sweetheart, Marta!"

That made me burst out laughing. "Yes, just imagine!"

He later confided to me that he had spent a long time pondering what he should say. "I was so terrified when I got home, because I hadn't managed to say anything!"

He met me again at two o'clock. The following day we

ran into Henrik on Pilestrædet. Otto rushed toward him, saying, "Congratulate us, old boy!"

We took a walk together every day after school, and in the evening I would go to meet Otto at his office. We agreed that we would get married during the summer holidays. Otto had eighteen hundred kroner, and I would keep my position as a schoolteacher. It was all going to be splendid.

I WAS TAKEN COMPLETELY BY SURPRISE. But not by Otto. Rushing springs had opened up in the very core of my being. I sat and listened in rapt amazement to the new music during those long evenings after we had said good night to each other and I was home. I simply sat and listened.

Back then, the fact that we were so different was something that I viewed as a joy. I walked around in a state of perpetual, delighted astonishment that the two of us, who were so different, had found each other.

Our school's drawing teacher was engaged to one of my former classmates. She came to visit me in my lodgings and plagued me to death with her talk of love.

"Oh, but isn't it wonderful? Oh, to have someone who understands you completely. Someone you can talk to about everything—simply *everything!*"

She and her sweetheart would walk along Kirkeveien and talk about simply everything.

"You know what, Marta? In my opinion trust has to exist if there's going to be anything *ideal* about love. If there's no true spiritual connection, what does the whole thing matter? Tell me that!"

"*L'amour sans phrase,*" I said and laughed smugly. Love without words.

"Desire is what I call it, pure and simple. And it's quite bestial—oh, forgive me!"

"I beg your pardon," I said and laughed even harder.

L'AMOUR SANS PHRASE. I walked around repeating that to myself when I was alone.

Love, love . . . There was nothing else in life that was worth living for. I loved so fanatically that it never seemed possible to immerse myself enough in my own love.

And I could feel how this love, day by day, made me beautiful and lively and radiant, giving me an unexpected awareness of life, making me bold and merry and infinitely superior.

Oh, I had been only a precocious child up until then, and suddenly I was young.

Everything I had read and everything I had learned continued to give me joy, but I also felt that such things were merely a means, not a goal. They were weapons good to have as I made my way through life. But love—that was life itself.

I felt so vital back then that I never doubted my own love or Otto's, or whether it was enough. I needed someone to love and who would love me—not a man who would "understand" me. Oh, how right I was then, with my contempt for the simple-minded, ill-mannered female howling for "understanding." Those women just wanted a man to be like a watchmaker, tending to their tedious, distorted little brains and wasting his time by coddling their vanity.

Oh, we women who feel misunderstood. We could probably go through an entire regiment of men, and it would still do little good. It's when the heart begins to wither, when we ourselves no longer understand, that we start to scream for understanding.

In those days I understood Otto. I didn't fully recognize how clearly I saw him exactly the way he was. I demanded nothing from him that he wasn't capable of giving. He hadn't grown up in a home among anemic academics, or lived among Aunt Guletta's mahogany furniture and beadwork. His father was a lumber dealer, and he was a businessman with all his heart and soul. He was also an athlete and outdoorsman and felt at home in his childhood surroundings, where I walked, enjoying the atmosphere and lighting, up there in "our" woods. Fresh air and sunshine flooded over me as I sat with my books, and God knows I pushed them aside and ran out into the bright world.

I don't think any man was ever more gentle or kind toward a young girl he loved than Otto was in the midst of our ungovernable love. And that's the way he has been in all the years that we've lived together.

If he had suspected that I didn't think he understood me, I know he would have honestly and sincerely tried to meet me halfway: that is how exceedingly conscientious Otto is. Yet since he never did anything to hinder me, but, on the contrary, thought everything that I was interested in was so splendid—women's rights and public education, and the like—he naturally assumed that everything was fine. He admired me as "furiously intelligent," just as he admires everything that he loves: the children and me, Henrik, his parents and siblings, his home, garden, and cabin, everything that's part of his world.

Later I grew annoyed with his constant, uncritical admiration of everything that belonged to him. But it was back then that I was right, when I saw only how handsome he was in his lively trust and joy.

Never mind that many a time he judged harshly and took a narrow-minded view when he didn't understand something. He was vigorous and kind and strong, and then it's easy to look only at the surface and not see deeper. Now I take a more lenient view of many things, but that's because I too am guilty. When I was young and innocent I was a harsher judge.

We keep learning all our lives—but God help us what we learn. To understand everything is supposed to mean to forgive everything; if so, then may God spare me from those people who forgive too much. That's merely something we say to console ourselves when life starts to leave its mark on us, and we have done various things that we would have been ashamed of in our better days. Or else we don't have the courage and energy to live according to our own temperament, and so we relinquish some of our demands. But in the long run a person receives in accordance with what he demands. The young are single-minded. For them there is only one path to salvation, and if they are any good, that's the road they take. Later you catch sight of other paths, and you think that one is in fact just as good as the other. Then you sit down and say: they're all much the same. It's easy to put the blame on tolerance and understanding when you no longer feel like doing anything with your life. But it takes single-mindedness and tenacity to achieve something, because aspirations are required, and that is the way of youth.

July 20, 1902

Today I sent the boys away for the first time. They're going to stay with their Aunt Helene for a month. They looked so sweet in their new blue Norfolk jackets that I had made for them with all those pockets.

After we saw them off on the train, Ingrid and I went to visit Otto. I wanted to show him the little girl who looked so lovely. I had to console her a bit because she didn't get to travel, and so she was allowed to wear her rose-colored dress with red bows in her shiny, copper-red curls. She looks good enough to eat, her skin is so radiant. I can hardly stop once I've started kissing her slender white neck, which vanishes inside the pink neckline of her dress. And those pretty lips and those big, light-brown eyes . . .

She bustled and scurried around us as Otto and I sat on a bench in the park and talked. He was in very good spirits today.

Never before has the view from up there been as beautiful as it was today. Maybe it was because of the sun. This miserable summer with its endless rain can make even healthy people feel ill. Below us the town and the big, open green slopes down near the fjord and the enclosing embrace of the low ridge of mountains, but so vast that it doesn't feel confining. Today the fjord was quite bright, like silver, and a damp mist hovered over everything.

As we sat there, Otto and I, and he put his arm around me, the two of us slipped into a wistful feeling of happiness, gentle and delicate.

"I can't help believing that we're going to be together again," said Otto. "I can feel how much better I'm getting every day. You and me and the children, Marta."

I had the same thought. I have a husband and children, after all. An infinite amount of joy and riches still awaits me. No doubt there will be difficult and trying times for us now that Otto is getting well—but so what? I think I'll be happy just to be allowed to work and toil—and know that I *can* work for my beloved family. They will never know how far away from them I once strayed. I think that the memory of my confused wandering in a desolate and hopeless land, and the memory of the shame I brought upon myself, will gradually fade and sink to the bottom of my soul. It taught me something: that I must protect with ceaseless devotion every opportunity for warmth and happiness in our home. I have paid with the dearest of lessons, but not in vain. A woman's purity is not merely a cliché: it's an infinitely precious treasure. I know that now. Maybe now I'll be able to give the others more than I ever could before; maybe I'll be more attentive to every little stirring in their souls—most of all in the children.

WHEN I WAS A YOUNG GIRL I always thought that being a mother must be the greatest thing in the world. I thought it was so marvelous that when it happened to me, I could hardly believe it. When I was expecting Einar, I felt so overwhelmed that I was almost ashamed, because it really was as though there were nothing else in the world. The child I was carrying filled my thoughts night and day. I was determined to take it all very sensibly and naturally—good Lord, it's what happens to every female, after all. Yet I also dreaded it terribly. I wanted it so much, with every fiber of my being, even if I had to die.

Although I love my children as dearly as any mother does, and although I think that I've loved them with such warmth and kept watch over every little development of their lives, there are still so many details that Otto noticed before I did, traits peculiar to each of them that he called to my attention. It's true that I've also had interests other than my children, but I feel absolutely positive that those interests have never robbed them of the slightest bit of my care. That didn't happen until I started to become so self-absorbed, examining what was missing from my own happiness. And they love me in return, more than most children love their parents, I think. Yet the relationship between them and Otto is much more spontaneous. I suppose that's because he's a more spontaneous person.

And they are so like him—Einar to such a degree that it's comical, even in his mannerisms. I noticed so plainly his energy yesterday and today. He wanted to pack his own things and Halfred's too, and when he stuffed the tickets and coin purse and handkerchief and padlocks into his pockets and repeated my instructions on what they were supposed to do when they changed trains in Hamar, he looked just like a miniature Otto.

Halfred doesn't resemble his father as much. Nor does he have red hair. "He's your son," says Otto. "He's always pondering the nature of things." At any rate, he's constantly asking questions, often about the oddest things, and he always wants to know "but why?" If I tell him not to ask so many questions, he only says, "But why shouldn't I, Mother?"

Åse also resembles Otto. That makes me very uncomfortable. I've read about something like that in a French novel, but I didn't think it was possible.

July 21, 1902

I went to visit Otto early today. We went out and sat on the same bench as yesterday. And as we were sitting there, along came Henrik.

He wanted to talk to Otto about something to do with the business. I got up to leave, but of course Otto wouldn't hear of it. He said I might as well stay there and then go back to town with Henrik.

So all three of us walked along the garden path, talking. Otto had his arm in mine, and Henrik walked on the other side of me. Otto was cheerful and boisterous and complained that he was getting fat. "And here's Marta, who always falls for thin people. I suppose you won't want to be seen with me anymore, will you?"

I can't help feeling furious that Henrik is able to keep himself under such tight control. That he can walk along and talk in such a natural manner with me and Otto.

Now I'm almost as unhappy as I was before. I had worked my way into a quietly joyous state of hope as I immersed myself in all the memories of our love. I had started to believe in the future. Then Henrik shows up. And he's going to be part of any future. I can't imagine how I could possibly avoid him.

July 22, 1902

Otto didn't view our relationship the same way I did, back then. For me it was merely eroticism, but for him it was also a terribly serious responsibility.

I don't think it ever occurred to me to tell him how I had lived my life before I met him, or what my thoughts or opinions had been. On those occasions when we talked about such things, it was Otto who initiated the discussion.

"Listen, Marta," Otto said one day. "I'm not a Christian, per se."

I remember that this was on a Sunday in early March. We were skiing in Nordmarken. Brilliant sunshine and the forest heavy with snow. In front of us was a small white meadow, a bog, crisscrossed with ski tracks. In the shadows the snow was deep violet. We sat down to rest and ate oranges. Right across from us a creek murmured beneath the ice, and the trees all around were completely covered with frost. Some were entirely frozen in thick, clear blocks of ice. I had pointed out to Otto a frozen sapling, asking him whether he thought it would ever sprout leaves again, and that's what we had been talking about.

"Not a Christian, per se" was, by the way, an excellent way of putting it. He explained what he believed and didn't believe in an earnest tone of voice, as if he expected to be contradicted. He thought it served no purpose for the pastors to come and demand that you should believe, just believe in everything it said in the Bible and then you would be saved. And if you used your common sense, you were condemned. You were supposed to believe in such things as the story of the devil creeping around among the apple trees and duping people into stealing, or the idea that God told Noah how he should build and tar his ship.

It was Otto's common sense that had rebelled. He refused to believe what others taught him without questioning anything. In fact, he criticized them rather sharply.

But to view Christianity as a religion in the same way as he viewed all other religions had never occurred to him. He concluded by saying: "But I do believe in God, of course."

"Well, I don't," I said.

I proceeded to explain what I believed and didn't believe: not in any kind of personal God, because "the world is much too unjust."

"I've often thought the same thing," said Otto. He was lying on his side in the snow and looking up at me, almost shocked.

"The world is much too big, Otto, and we're too small. And life doesn't take us into consideration."

"Don't you believe in eternal life, then?" asked Otto quietly.

"No."

That evening, as we ended our day of skiing the way we ended all our excursions, with Otto having tea up in my room, he started talking about this topic again. He stayed much longer than usual—he, who was normally so meticulous about leaving at a "suitable hour." When he left, he said, "Actually, I don't think it's good that you know so much more than I do, Marta."

I felt a little ashamed after he left. We might never have talked about this topic—maybe not until after we were married. And this was partially because I had, in a way, underestimated Otto with the arrogance of the middle class toward a country boy. I'd witnessed a little of this in the relationship between Henrik and Otto; in many areas my cousin felt that he alone was entitled to an opinion, and he would practically brush Otto aside whenever he expressed his own view. Now that suddenly made me angry. We had no right to do that, neither he nor I. Oh, the stupid snobbishness of a graduate, scornful that Otto was "only" a businessman. That's the way I had described him in my mind—as prelude to my joy over the splendid, wonderful outdoorsman, that strapping fellow. But on that evening I was ashamed because I had never taken the time to find out his thoughts.

I felt this even more strongly on another occasion later on.

This was shortly before our wedding. We had gone to see the apartment, and I remember that Otto was preoccupied with what we called the "Turkish corner," which had a low bench fastened to the wall and a little table. There we would drink our coffee, and there were going to be tapestries covering the wall behind.

"Blue," said Otto. "A proper, vivid cornflower blue. And lots of cushions in all shades of blue. Blue, that's the color that suits you best."

It had rained in the afternoon, and now, toward evening, the air was as humid and warm as in a greenhouse and saturated with the scent of flowers. The whole town was fragrant with chestnut blossoms and lilacs, and as we headed up Kirkeveien, it was quite overwhelming—that bitter smell of birch leaves and the scent from the flower gardens. I could distinctly make out the delicate perfume of peonies, reminiscent of polished wooden objects from Japan, but even stronger were the chestnuts and lilacs. I remember noticing how lovely the pale lavender lilacs looked against the heavy, blue-gray clouds that were retreating eastward.

I think the world was more beautiful that evening than I've ever seen it since. We reached the hill across from Vestre Aker parsonage. In the late afternoon sun everything was golden: the tufts of cloud in the blue sky and the gnats hovering over the creek below and the willow trees along the road. The meadow glistened with moisture in the sunlight, as did the crowns of the trees, dripping with sparkling droplets, as well as the old blue tile roof of the parsonage. Over the garden fence hung white lilacs, and the telephone wires ran past, glittering gold, like the strings of a great golden harp.

We went into the grove across from the parsonage. It has always been one of my favorite places, that little grove on the Blindern estate with the walled cemetery up on the hill. Back then I thought the circular stone enclosure looked like the ruins of a castle, and in the delicate grass beneath the leafy trees grew the fragile, pale green herbs called moschatel.

We sat on a rock where a sort of grass-covered lane leads up to the graves.

Otto had been quiet all afternoon. He sat there with his elbows propped on his knees and his head resting in his hands, and neither of us spoke for a long time. Then he said softly: "You know . . . there *is* one thing. I think . . . I know that it's my duty to tell you this."

He paused and then said: "I have . . . I'm not . . . I've . . . I've known other women, you see . . . before."

After a moment, he said, "I can imagine that you find this horrifying . . . I can tell from looking at you. I know that's what you must think. And I couldn't make myself tell you before. You don't understand it, of course, and I can't explain it . . . not because I want to make excuses . . ."

I tried to say something, but he interrupted me.

"Not in the past couple of years. Not since my sister Lydia died. You know, Mrs. Jensen. She had such an unhappy marriage. Then I promised myself certain things. But before that . . . It's not something you can understand. When a person is younger, then it's not . . ."

"Otto, you mustn't tell me anything more!"

"Do you think it's *that* terrible?" he said, standing up.

Then I stood up, too. What I felt was merely confusion and shame for myself. At first, when he began to speak, I was filled with enormous astonishment. It wasn't something I'd ever thought about, at least not since we had become engaged. A year or two earlier I might well have discussed the question of what a man should admit to, etc. It was a topic avidly debated at the time, and I would have been within my rights. But as he talked and I saw how pained he felt, and how awfully serious this was for him, I felt so ashamed and humbled that I hardly dared look up. I thought that never, ever had my love for him been anything more than a wish that he would think I was lovely and kiss and pamper me, that I could put my hands on his broad shoulders. But never had I looked for his soul, seeking to treat it with kindness and love.

"No, no, Otto. You mustn't say another word. My dear, what right do I have to demand such a thing from you? It has never, ever occurred to me to give you an account of the bad things I've done or still do—my ugly, evil, petty thoughts or deeds. I haven't even begun to think about how much I will have to change in myself now that we're going to be married."

"You? Oh, Marta, Marta . . ."

"Tell me everything if you *want* to tell me. I know that I'll be able to understand you . . . now. Everything that you want someone else to know and discuss with you—I *beg* you to tell me all that. But there's nothing I demand to know or think I have the right to ask you about. Because we know that we can depend on each other, and we are terribly, terribly fond of each other—aren't we?"

"Oh, I can't tell you how much I love you—that you can take it like this!"

Then we walked, close to each other, up and down the old wet lane where the raindrops fell and glittered the whole time, and I was unspeakably happy and a little ashamed that Otto thought I was being so splendid.

"Yes, after we're married, dear," said Otto, and with that we kissed until we could hardly breathe. And as we headed back home, I felt a superior sense of compassion for all the other couples we encountered.

OTTO'S FATHER AND BROTHER-IN-LAW came to the wedding. My father-in-law was not particularly pleased with the arrangements we had made. He had wanted us to go up to Løiten and hold the wedding there, since my own parents were dead. We had been to Auli during Easter, but it wasn't very pleasant. Even though they were very kind to me, I could tell that they would have preferred Otto to marry a girl with money, and they found me too "refined," although God knows I tried to be as reserved and modest as I possibly could. But Otto was sweet and thoughtful and took great pains so that I wouldn't notice any ill will, which made me enjoy the trip in spite of everything. And Helene, my sister-in-law, was one of the sweetest persons imaginable.

We had a civil ceremony, and then I hosted a dinner at the Grand Hotel. Two of my girlfriends had made the arrangements, and it was quite a success, so that my father-in-law and Tomas Nordås were in very good spirits before Otto and I left.

When I went to my room to change out of my good blue suit and patent-leather boots, my landlady had already started clearing things out. She had removed the linens from the bed, and the tablecloth had been folded and placed on a corner of the table. My own belongings were piled in one corner; they were to be taken over to our apartment that evening.

I shed a few tears, feeling a bit sentimental as I changed my clothes. Then Otto appeared as I was standing there, fastening my shirtwaist. He forgot to knock.

"Oh, pardon me, but you'd better hurry. It's almost four, you know."

He started repacking my knapsack, taking several things out of it and putting them into his own bag. He picked up some underclothes, and I saw him turn slightly red.

"You've brought along enough stockings, haven't you?" he said and buckled the straps.

Then we hurried up Maridalsveien in the brilliant sunlight. Otto's grocer, Helgesen on Sandakerveien, was going to drive us to Nitedal.

There was something rustic and festive about Helgesen's property that reminded me of all the good times in my childhood, with the stalls and storerooms all around, the pump in the center of the courtyard, and the doves on the roof.

"Well, I was just about to give up on the two of you," said Helgesen. "Oh, so this is your missus, Oulie? She's a tiny one, and pretty too, that she is." He congratulated me with a strong handshake.

Otto chatted with Helgesen a bit as we drove, talking about people in Nitedal and Maridal I didn't know. To me it sounded so peaceful and pleasant. The city seemed unreal and far away. On the farms around Maridal Lake, the hay had been gathered in stacks. In some places they were taking the hay in, and in other places they were just starting to cut the rye. From the other side of the lake came the clanking sound of a reaper, and Otto and Helgesen eagerly and earnestly talked about the prospects for the year. As we drove into the forest, Otto took my hand and squeezed it, but we didn't speak.

"Well, have a good time, the two of you. Farewell, Oulie, farewell, Madame!" Helgesen grinned as he dropped us off.

We didn't say much as we walked along the forest path. Otto looked back at me a couple of times, to ask if he was going too fast, and made some remark or other about how many trees had been toppled by the wind—the path was often entirely blocked—and about how wet it was in the marshes now. Once he picked a handful of white orchids and gave them to me.

"Aren't they pretty? Pin them to your blouse. They would look good there."

It was getting late, and the sunlight was golden up along the rim of the ridge. Here and there a ray of sun fell across the path as we walked at the foot of a cliff along a small rushing river. The sun glinted on the spray and on the wet birches and elderberry bushes. Bluebells and monkshood were everywhere.

"Oh, how magnificent they are," I said, and Otto turned around.

"Do you like them? Yes, they're beautiful. There are lots of them right below the cabin," said Otto. "Well now, that's a fine thing. The footbridge is washed out."

We had reached a little waterfall. At that point the river was wide and deep, and there was only a single round log for a bridge.

"Give me your hand," said Otto. "But dear, sweet Marta—what is it?"

My heart was pounding so hard that I was shaking, and I could feel that my face had turned white. My hand was ice-cold.

"But my dear, are you frightened?" whispered Otto.

I threw my arms around his neck and hid my face. It wasn't really fear; it was more like a physical tension. When at the same moment my foot landed in a marshy hole and water seeped in over the edge of my boot, my whole body seemed to freeze. My skin contracted, and I felt so naked in my clothes.

"We're almost there," whispered Otto. "It's just up this ridge."

It was a steep slope.

"All right," said Otto as he stopped to catch his breath.

Below us, down a sheer drop, lay a big, gleaming lake. And some distance away, on a little green rise in the midst of the setting sun, stood a small gray hut. We came to a split-rail fence, and Otto moved the logs aside.

"So now we're home," said Otto, putting his arms around me. He kissed me, and I sensed it was different from any of the kisses he had given me. It was a kiss of welcome. We walked across the embankment. There was a profusion of violets and wild pansies, and in every pile of stones grew monkshood and fireweed. The lake below us gleamed among the birch trees and alder thickets.

On the stoop we found a bucket of milk and a basket of potatoes. A huge bouquet of wildflowers lay next to them.

Otto opened the door and let me enter first into the dimly lit room.

WE STAYED ONLY TWO WEEKS AT THE CABIN. That was the extent of Otto's summer vacation. And God knows, it passed quickly enough. Yet when I think back on those days, I see a thousand happy memories.

I remember one night when I woke at the gray light of dawn. First I sat in bed for a long time, looking at Otto, and I felt almost scared at being so happy. I couldn't make myself lie down and go back to sleep.

Finally I got up and, with only a shawl over my night-gown, I sat on the stoop and looked at the mild, hazy morning.

I had been sitting there for a long time when Otto suddenly called me.

"My dear . . . why are you sitting out there? Are you already up?"

With a sudden feeling, rather like shame—or fear at disclosing something that I wasn't sure he would under-stand—I told him that I had gotten up to make coffee to bring to him in bed.

"Oh, God save me. What an amazing energy you have all of a sudden—and what a wife you are, too. So wake me when it's ready," said Otto, and he lay back down to sleep.

ONE EVENING WE GOT LOST. It was as dark as a summer night can be when we came to a big marsh that we didn't recognize.

"The smartest thing would be for us to stay right here," said Otto. "Would you be awfully afraid to sleep outdoors for one night?"

I thought it would be splendid. I had never spent a whole night outdoors before.

We made a narrow bed for ourselves among the blueberry tussocks. Otto wrapped his sweater and my jacket around our feet, and then I lay down with my head on his shoulder and looked up at the sky, which was a pale blue even though it was quite late, and at the mountain right across from us, which was outlined black and sharp against the yellowish-white horizon. The delicate pale yellow glow that moved along the edge of the sky, eastward, was reflected in the pools of water on the marsh.

Occasionally we would doze off, then chat for a bit. Suddenly Otto said: "Dear, when the two of us have a little boy, his name will be Einar. I had a brother by that name."

He had mentioned this brother once before, when we were visiting Auli at Easter. I had seen the family gravesite near the church, and Otto told me that Einar had died when he was accidentally shot.

Now he lay there, talking about his brother, their

childhood, about that winter afternoon when they were ski-ing on the mountain and Einar took an entire load of buck-shot to the thigh. How they struggled to bind the wound but couldn't stop the bleeding, and then his leg began to freeze off as they dragged him down on his skis.

"Then Andreas, our friend, started crying. We couldn't get him to stop. And we didn't know exactly where we were, either—just the general direction—but as you probably re-alize, we didn't have much time. I remember that there were so many stars out that night, with bright moonlight and new snow on the icy crust. And how I prayed to God—and felt so small.

"But you know, on a night like tonight, I feel just as small. I thought about what you said. If there is a God, my dear, then we're lying here before him like two little mice in a hollow."

I pressed myself closer to him, in quiet, delighted amazement at hearing him say exactly what I was thinking just then.

We went up to the cabin every Sunday until late into the autumn.

That was before it became so common to have a cabin. Ours was just an old crofter's cottage. Back then, before we rebuilt it, there was only a kitchen with a fireplace and a four-poster bed, and no furniture other than what had been left behind by the crofter, plus two or three folding chairs that Otto had transported up there and lots of pots for flow-ers. Otto loves flowers and has his own way of arranging them. All he has to do is put a couple of flowers in a cup, and they look beautiful.

We kept adding improvements over the summer: embroidered tablecloths and a sofa with cushions under the window.

In the main room there was a stove where we cooked. Otto was the chef. He claimed I wasn't good at making anything and took over all the cooking in his shirtsleeves.

"Marta, my dear, what a hopeless creature you are!"

EVERY EVENING we would walk to Lillerud for milk. Otto was best friends with everybody over there, and I was immediately taken into the family. On those long cool evenings I would lie on the embankment and talk to Ragna and the children, while from up on the ridge we heard the bells of horses wandering freely in the forest. And I would listen for Otto's voice as he sat on the steps and talked to Mother—Ragna's mother—and Ragna's husband.

Life up in the forest made our relationship happy and harmonious. A tender and joyous intimacy would arise of its own accord as we spent days roaming in the woods, picking berries—climbing over heaps of raspberries among lush ferns, where I was afraid of snakes, and where cowberries blushed red on old gray tree stumps, or hiking along shadowy blueberry slopes with golden rays of sun on velvety soft moss, plodding through marshes where Otto dashed about, picking the scarce and tiny cloudberries, which he instantly presented to me, all of them. Then he would describe the abundance of cloudberries there used to be back home, and we'd end up telling each other all kinds of things about our childhood and youth—eventually everything. Otto knew practically every road and path in all of Nitedal and Nordmarken. He knew every bird song and the habits of every animal, and about weather portents and stars and such things. After all, he'd been roaming around in those forests and meadows ever since he was a tyke. And out there I was simply Otto's little girl, and he took such care of me.

THE SMALL BUILDING that was our first home has been torn down. I'm almost glad about that now; it would have been painful to walk past and see other people living inside. But on that evening several years ago when Otto and I walked by and saw that they had begun demolishing the place, we stopped and looked at each other. I started to cry, and Otto seemed just as sad as I was. The house was empty and the garden fence had been torn down. Several of the trees lay toppled onto the raspberry bushes that Otto had planted. We went into the garden. The veranda door stood open, so we went inside and wandered through the empty rooms. All the windowpanes had been removed. We didn't say much, not even as we walked home. We were both feeling sad, as if we had lost a beloved refuge for our thoughts. That was back when I was so dissatisfied with my life, and I thought it seemed symbolic that they were tearing down and destroying the place where I had once been so happy.

When we got home, Otto went into the garden, where

he puttered around, tending to the roses, which he had just wrapped up against the frost. This was late in the fall. When I came onto the veranda to call him for supper, he said in such a sad voice: "We should have taken all the roses with us when we moved. It's such a pity what's happened to them. And my raspberries—just when they were starting to get big."

IT WASN'T A VERY FANCY HOUSE, our first one, but Lord, it was cozy. The house had once been a coachman's residence or something similar for a country estate and later a wooden veranda had been added to one side. The house stood at the end of a cul-de-sac, which Otto called the "appendix." The branches of the maple trees in the yard seemed almost to meet overhead. It was unbelievably muddy in the spring and fall. The children always looked like pigs when they came inside, but I didn't have the heart to scold them. I often would have liked to be a child myself, making cakes out of the greasy black mud and running a grocery store from a board laid across two bricks.

What odd things Otto would bring home! It's true that I often thought they were terribly ugly, all those urns and vases of his. But I was touched that he was trying to be inventive in order to please me and decorate our house, which made him so proud. He was always up early, and while I got dressed he would rush in and out, telling me which roses were now in full bloom or that he had picked radishes for breakfast.

In many ways he was quite childish. During our engagement, he had tried to hide this from me. Back then he was also very afraid of seeming naive or provincial. After we were married, he wasn't the least bit embarrassed about this anymore—just as I could no longer hide how in love I was with him. And he would frequently use his boyishness to flirt with me. Among other things, he had a penchant for making remarks that were slightly risqué, but always in such an innocent and youthful manner. For example, he never grew tired of joking that it was actually unseemly that our maid's name was Olerine, which gave rise to vile images of "cholérine."

He was immensely amused by my school stories. One Sunday we invited my whole class over for hot chocolate. Otto was a splendid host for nineteen girls and teased them until we were completely giddy, all twenty of us. After that the class was utterly smitten with "the teacher's Pappa." That was during the second year of our marriage, when Einar was only a few months old.

Lord, how I boasted about that child. But Otto was even worse. And how he pampered me the entire time before the birth. The poor man. While I was convalescing, he had bought a hanging lamp. It was supposed to be a surprise for after my confinement, but he couldn't resist telling me about it long before, and he carried me into the room, wrapped in a woolen blanket, so I could see it.

Whenever I hear the sound of a lawnmower, it makes me think of the summer when Einar was a baby. I would sit on the veranda in a drowsy state, with a book or some mending and watch Otto as he labored, in his shirtsleeves, with a perspiring face. He cut the grass at least every other day with an old lawnmower he had bought at an auction. He had an arsenal of garden tools under the veranda steps, enough to keep the grounds of a palace neat and tidy. The clattering of the lawnmower sounded so peaceful and summery, and I would sit there and doze until Otto came over to ask me to wipe his brow, give him some lemonade, or come down and look at his eight cauliflower plants and the cucumbers. And Einar would lie in the sunshine, sleeping under the gauzy netting, pink and warm and lovely, with his sweet little hands that clutched my breast so wondrously whenever I nursed him.

I THINK IT ACTUALLY BEGAN as a kind of weariness. I had become sated with happiness. I've read somewhere that happiness is always the same. And it was.

Halfred was born, and I started teaching again. The baby was incorporated into our daily life with the whole apparatus of chores, routines, and considerations that are part of any type of household and yet create a home. As far as Otto was concerned, all the exact same feelings arose— everything that had occurred after Einar's birth was now repeated. The first time his response had made me happy, but now I thought it was all a little comical, a bit pathetic, and it offended me slightly. Good Lord, I thought. Then Otto wanted me to stop teaching. His own business, which he had started by then, was flourishing. That was during the good period. We also belonged to quite a large social group, mostly Otto's business friends. I thought rather sadly that he was going to develop into a proper, narrow-minded citizen—he had that tendency—and I would lose my own circle of friends and my own interests, which I had always maintained a woman could hold on to if she had a husband and children. Then history would repeat itself, until I grew tired and ugly from all the children I was bound to have. In the end I would undoubtedly be reduced to nothing more than one of the entries in Otto Oulie's thick catalog of blessings.

None of this was crystal clear to me at the time, but it was the reason for my melancholy mood. As the relationship then existed between Otto and me, I felt there was a danger that we might drift apart. I clung to my work and to my children, as if wanting to have them in reserve should I suffer disappointment in what was still the most important aspect of my life.

Otto thought I was ill. He promptly summoned our family doctor, ordered me to drink wine and take iron tablets, wanted me to stay with Helene for a while or at our cabin, but in particular he wanted me to stop teaching after summer vacation. I didn't feel like doing anything. Actually, there was something new, interesting, and pleasant about sitting like that, sad and tired and brooding, especially when Otto would come in, sit with me, and worriedly indulge me.

"But my sweet little Marta, what's wrong with you? My dear, you mustn't be ill!"

"There's nothing wrong with me, Otto," I would tell him as I accepted his kisses. Maybe I was also hoping to bind him to me in that way.

WHEN IT WAS TIME for Otto's annual trip to London, he wanted to take me with him. I didn't want to go. First, because I couldn't really imagine leaving the children. And second . . . as a young girl I'd always had a great wish to go out and travel, but it had to be in such a way that I could live in each city, get to know the people, absorb the atmosphere of the place, learn about its uniqueness. This kind of trip would be completely different.

Well, of course I went along. And I had a splendid time. At first I woke up at night at the hour when I usually got up to check on the children, to see if they had thrown off the covers. Then I would feel sad at finding myself in a hotel room, and I would think about my little ones far away in Kristiania. But I missed them less than I had expected, which made me almost ashamed. Otto decided that we should go to Paris as well, and we spent a lovely week there. He conscientiously took me around to see everything a person should see: museums and theaters and a few places of entertainment that Otto enthusiastically viewed as the mysteries of Paris. And I bought a hat and a tailored suit and two sets of silk underclothes, as well as a dainty corset and silk slip, in which I danced the can-can for Otto when we got back to the hotel one morning at four a.m. and drank champagne in our room, each of us more eager than the other to tell everyone at home about our wild outings.

Then I was back home and started teaching again in good spirits. And for two peaceful years I was quite content with my life.

IN REALITY it was perhaps the sorriest of trifles that started it all.

We needed a larger apartment. We were already feeling so cramped that we could hardly breathe, and now I was expecting our third child, so we had to move. If we could have acquired the upstairs flat, too, we might have managed, and then everything might have turned out differently. But the carpenter and his family didn't want to move.

I was unhappy with the new apartment from the very beginning. I didn't like any of the accommodations that we looked at, and I wasn't feeling well, which made me angry, and this was in the autumn when the weather was terrible. And Otto had at least seven other apartments on his list, so I allowed myself to be persuaded by him and the landlord to end the search. But from the start I had made up my mind not to like our new home.

I thought the street was disgusting—a truly snobbish neighborhood with ugly little houses and desolate gardens with a gazebo in one corner, and you could tell that not a single person had ever sat there. Granite pillars at the building entrance, with a signboard of tedious tenant names, and cream-colored curtains and Majolica urns in the windows. A glimpse of the parlor revealed floor lamps and pedestals and palms and everything that was ugly.

Otto thought it was a charming neighborhood. And when I clung to his arm and acted in great pain, he merely said: "Well, how can you expect not to feel sick, Marta, when you *refuse* to do what the doctor says?"

Then we had to have more furnishings. The new apartment was exactly twice the size of the old one. Otto bought leather furniture for his smoking room, and we went around to look at "salon" furniture but couldn't agree. One evening we saw a large suite of furniture made of jacaranda wood in a department store window. Otto thought it was charming. "It's in the Russian style," he said. God knows where he had that from. I said that I thought the color was pretty. It was upholstered in turquoise crushed velvet. Otto behaved mysteriously for a week. Then one evening he dragged me over to the new apartment, and there stood the "Russian" furniture in all its splendor.

INGRID WAS BORN. No doubt Otto's deepest wish was fulfilled. He was so delighted with her and so infatuated that I almost felt annoyed. I thought it looked ridiculous to see that big tall man rushing around with her in his arms, murmuring baby talk. He would dash to the nursery the minute he came home from the office, even before he said hello to me.

"Little mother, here we come, the two of us!" And then he would shove the baby right into my face, without paying any attention to what I might be doing.

"Ugh, what's that you're sitting there reading now?" he might say. "To think you'd bother!"

"Oh, I'm just so sick and tired of that stupid baby, she smells so awful," Einar said one day when Otto was fussing with Baby Sister more than usual. Otto got mad, but I just laughed at Einar and pulled him onto my lap.

I STOPPED TEACHING FOR GOOD before Ingrid was born. Otto's business was now thriving, and we hadn't spent a lot of money during those first years. Otto wanted me to live comfortably, to have as much help in the house as I wanted, and the like. I started reading a great deal again, went to a few lectures that interested me, and joined several clubs and associations.

That didn't really please Otto. He never said anything directly to me, but when any of the women from my clubs would visit he would often be slightly ill-tempered and try to give the impression that he was a proper tyrant at home.

One day he was present as my friends and I drank tea and conversed. During a momentary lull he said, "Children, there *is* something that I've forgotten today. I wonder what it could be?"

And both boys shrieked delightedly in unison: "You must have forgotten to give Mamma a thrashing!"

"By Jove, you're right! Remind me about that tonight, won't you, Einar?"

All three of them were greatly amused. Then he grabbed each of the boys by the ear and hauled them away: "Let's us menfolk go into my study."

They raised quite a ruckus in his smoking room, sounding like wild animals.

ONE DAY AT NOON Otto came home with a puppy he had bought. It was a terrier and we named him Peik. All of us were utterly delighted with him. "I'd rather have Peik than Baby Sister," said Halfred.

Poor little Peik. We had him only six months before he was run over, and Otto had to put the dog out of his misery. He cried, the children cried, and I cried.

Then one day when I was getting dressed, Otto came to me and said vehemently: "I don't understand why you have to be so involved in all this stuff. Are you out of your mind, Marta? How can you? This time it was just a poor puppy. Next time it might be one of your own children!"

"Wait a minute, now you're really being too protective! But if you have something against the fact that I'm interested in such things—women's rights and the like—then I think you should tell me straight out!"

"You know quite well that I have nothing against those things. I think it's all very fine and justified and all that—but couldn't you just leave it to others for a while? As long as you have three children who are so young?"

"But good Lord, Otto, it could be a long time before I'm done with having babies!"

"Are you sorry about having children, Marta?"

"I'm not even going to answer that. But you certainly do whatever you can to make me sorry about having them."

"Now listen here, Marta—we menfolk have to tend to our jobs and our businesses, even though we might not have time for anything else. And when you women get married, you know what your work is going to be, as a rule. And I don't think it's such terribly boring work to take care of your own children and keep your home nice. So I don't feel very sorry for you women. And if you have to put your own interests aside for a while for that reason . . . well, that's no different from what men have to do, too. Good Lord, you don't think I have much time to devote to my own interests, do you?"

"At least you have your singing group," I said.

"One evening a week! Do you think that's too much?"

"No, God knows . . . if anything, it's too little," I said.

And we stood there quarreling.

August 7, 1902

Rain and more rain. A summer like this is enough to drive a person mad.

It's worse for Otto. He would, of course, get well quicker if only we had warm sunny weather. He is indisputably getting better, but very slowly, it seems to me. Even though the doctor sounds encouraging, I can't help feeling worried. It's probably just nerves—I've always been susceptible to letting the weather influence my mood. Poor Otto. Today he talked about almost nothing else but Nordmarken because I'd brought him flowers from Ragna. She came to visit me yesterday, and she asked about him and the children.

I spent all morning with Otto. In the afternoon I made paper cutouts for Ingrid—she's been bored to tears lately. When I came back from town, her toys, along with Åse's, were scattered all over the place, and the maid is and will always be impossible.

I don't like living here on Neuberggaden. But I know it's foolish to worry so much about all the outer circumstances— God knows I think I'm doing everything I can to battle my ill humor. But the neighborhood *is* appalling. All these half-finished streets and new houses that already look decrepit—these small apartments with their shabby-chic furnishings, set close together with tiny balconies, garishly painted stairwells, filthy entryways. In every other courtyard a delicatessen or a shoemaker's shop, and on every corner a new grocery store. Another one seems to open every week. And everybody here is so much the same. Each time a newly married couple moves in—and half the residents are newly married, while the other half have an income of about three or four thousand per year and six or eight children, and two-thirds of the women wear loose capes and are in the so-called "blessed" family way—they all have the same three suites of furniture: plush upholstered for the parlor, an oak dining set, and mahogany beds and chests of drawers. How awful to share a stairwell with eight families and the laundry room with sixteen, and to have a balcony that is visible from fifteen other ones here in the building, not to mention the neighboring buildings. And the rain has ruined all my flowers on the balcony, all my red geraniums, and I was so looking forward to bringing bouquets to Otto.

How lovely it would be to have a garden. I'll certainly appreciate it if we ever have one again. And a telephone!

It's actually not bad here for the children. The boys, at any rate, have a splendid time in all these construction sites and the half-finished streets. As for Ingrid and Åse, they mostly stay with the maid in the empty lot and dig in the sand. When I think about how things were for the boys when they were small . . . poor little Ingrid has nothing else to keep her busy except putting dirt in her red tin pail and then pouring it from one sand pile to the other. If only the weather were good enough so that she could do this every day, things would be fine. Although God save me, what a trial it is with all the laundry in the kitchen.

August 10, 1902

I feel so horribly lost and confused, especially at night when I lie in bed, longing for Otto up at Grefsen, and missing Einar and Halfred, who are at Løiten. Sometimes I take Åse into my bed all night long so I won't feel so alone.

It's better in the daytime. Then I'm always thinking up all kinds of plans for the future. But when I truly consider the life that we're going to start, then I can be almost feverish with impatience. Good Lord, good Lord, how long is this going to continue? My heart feels like it will burst. Then Otto asks me what's wrong. He can always tell now whenever something is wrong. It's strange how his illness has made him so perceptive. He notices at once every little change in my mood. I've never loved my husband as much as I do now.

THEN HENRIK CAME HOME from England. He had inherited money from one of his uncles, and he and Otto became business partners.

I HAD ACTUALLY LOST TOUCH with Henrik after I became engaged. He went to England at about the same time Otto and I were married, and found an excellent position there. We visited him when we were in London, and he and Otto corresponded a bit. Occasionally I would add a greeting to Otto's letters and receive in turn congratulations on my birthday or whenever Otto told him about an addition to our family.

During the time when they were making arrangements for the new company, it was natural for Henrik to come to our house quite often, and the three of us also did a great deal of socializing together, going to the theater and eating supper out and the like.

Otto admired Henrik beyond words. In the beginning I was happy to have him visit, mostly because it somehow brought Otto and me closer together.

The three of us would talk about all kinds of things.

Henrik has always been fond of talking. And we aired our ideas as we used to do in the old days, at Aunt Guletta's house and in Henrik's lodgings. Naturally, things were quite different now—if only because of the fact that now we all had had experiences that served as a basis for our discussions. So we talked somewhat less. And Henrik had grown quite reserved. But he has always been exceptionally good at giving brief but articulate speeches on all sorts of topics.

I think he wanted to lend us a helping hand. He knew both of us quite well, but he stood outside of us, looking in at our home, and he clearly grasped the situation at once.

He was the one who steered the conversation to subjects that indirectly touched on our relationship, always in general terms. All three of us pretended that we weren't talking about ourselves. Yet Otto and I were able to say so much to each other, and Henrik would agree with first one and then the other of us, presenting the issues so that we both became aware of much that we hadn't previously understood, since we were right in the midst of it all.

In a sense, it was a kind of settling of accounts—or a clearing of the air. And I can't deny that when things had been cleared out, I felt a bit empty inside.

That was a dangerous feeling. I was living so comfortably, and I had too much time to think about myself. Otto, being the kind of person that he is, was affected in such a way that he was even more considerate toward me than before. For many years he had taken charge of my life for me, without thinking that I might not be so enthusiastic about the home and the circle of friends and the routines that he had arranged for both of us. It never occurred to him that my opinions were anything more than "whims," and he didn't have time to pay attention to them because he was simply too busy trying to provide all those comforts for me.

Now he suddenly heard the same opinions voiced by Henrik. I think most men listen more closely to a friend whom they also highly respect than to the wife they have been married to for eight to ten years. That was true of Otto, at any rate.

Another matter was that my self-confidence grew as I became the focus of Henrik's attentiveness and empathy. I had always felt a slight admiration for him because he was handsome and articulate. Now, having returned from abroad, he was something of a novelty, and it was rather intriguing to renew our old, familiar relationship. Rumor had it that he had "lived" a great deal during those years—in all senses of the word. Otto hinted as much, and the women in our social circle spoke with great zeal about it. They found Henrik wildly interesting and sweet and were exceedingly impressed. And I had become enough a part of their group that I was more influenced by their views than I even knew.

AND SO I DRIFTED quite passively with the current, nursing my moods.

HENRIK HAD FURNISHED a charming bachelor's home in a garret apartment on Munkedamsveien. Otto and I frequently spent our evenings there, with me sitting on the old corner sofa or on the balcony, talking to Henrik, who showed me his maps and art objects, while Otto sat at the piano. Back then he was quite diligent about his music, taking lessons from Mrs. Onarheim and practicing difficult pieces. For me, those evenings in Henrik's quiet, stylish rooms were sheer pleasure.

"What a damned elegant place Henrik has, my dear," said Otto one evening as we walked home. "It's certainly different, for example, from . . . our home."

"Yes," I said. "Well, you're the one who has to take credit for our place. So if you don't like it, then . . ."

"Good heavens! Of course our home is charming, and comfortable, too. I just meant that it's not as . . . original as Henrik's." After a moment he added, "I'm not accustomed to paying attention to such things, you know. But actually, I can't understand it, Marta. I would have thought that you, of all people, could have created a home that was equally stylish."

I DON'T EVEN KNOW what we had argued about that afternoon. Some trivial matter. But I was feeling churlish because I'd had a difficult time getting the children properly dressed for a party. We were sitting on the balcony, drinking coffee, and I was acting stubborn, so Otto finally exclaimed:

"Forgive me, damn it, but surely you must admit that there's *something* that you don't know better than everyone else!"

Henrik arrived at that moment, and right afterward the merchant Høidahl's children arrived to play with ours. I had often been annoyed by Otto's naive admiration for these upper-class offspring, especially for the precocious little ladies over in Westend. He seemed to feel honored that his children were allowed to play with them. Now he was perched on the veranda railing, listening to little Judith give an account of all the dances she had attended during the winter. I found it amusing to hear the girl boast and make up things, but Otto listened with obvious interest.

At that instant Halfred screamed. He and Einar had apparently gotten into a fight, and Otto rushed inside to see what was going on.

As he ran off, Henrik and I looked at each other and smiled. And there was something in that smile that made me feel ashamed of myself. I sensed that Henrik felt the same. In my own defense, I started talking—for the first time directly about my relationship with Otto. It was practically an indictment of my husband. "He doesn't *see* anything," I said, trying to make excuses for him. But it *was* an indictment.

"No, he doesn't see that you're different," said Otto's friend, and he too attempted to muster some sort of defense, but it sounded strangely half-hearted.

Otto came back. He stood next to my chair, kissed me, and pulled me to my feet.

"Don't you think Marta looks nice in this dress? Isn't she charming?"

That was to make me forget that he had lost his temper. Then he left.

"Well, congratulations on the new dress," said Henrik and looked at me for a moment. Then he quickly looked away.

But not quickly enough. I'd heard how strange his voice sounded, and my heart gave a leap. He's in love with me! I thought.

I didn't think anything of it, except that I found it amusing. A naive seventeen-year-old couldn't have been more insensitive, or rejoiced in a more cynical fashion.

I flirted with Henrik that evening, consciously and even quite openly. I had a nail in my shoe that was hurting me, and I kicked off the shoe and asked Henrik to pound the nail in with a rock. He did as I asked and then handed the shoe back to me.

"How elegant you look," said Henrik. "Do you wear silk stockings every day?"

"Otto gives me so many pairs," I said. "He acquired a taste for them in Paris." And I told him about dancing the can-can for Otto.

Henrik looked as if he had swallowed something bitter. "You really ought to try that again."

"I don't think it would help matters now," I said. We were strolling back and forth in the garden. "There's a time and place for everything—that's what Otto thinks, you see. *He*, at least, is done with the can-can. Now we're supposed to live pleasantly in our cozy home. And if I don't find it pleasant, that's too bad for me, because he doesn't even notice. It's not that he doesn't think about me, because he most certainly does, but he thinks of me as his own particular possession."

And once again we were talking about Otto.

"He actually thinks much more about others than about himself," said Henrik. "But the others have to belong to him in some manner. That's also why he works so hard, because in a way he's working for himself—and for those who belong to him. I don't think he would be capable of doing work for the sake of the work alone. He would give his life at once, and gladly, for you or the children—but for some cause? Never!"

A lowly crofter! The phrase raced through my mind. And then I instantly thought: no, you have no right to say that. How ugly and mean—shame on you. I tried to erase the phrase, but not its effect. I wanted to look down on Otto for a bit.

"Poor man, he tries to fulfill everyone's wishes so swiftly that they hardly even have time to make a wish," said Henrik. "And it never occurs to him that anyone might wish for something different from what he does. You see, he forgot long ago that you weren't *born* Marta Oulie."

"Henrik," I said. "Sometimes I wish that he wasn't so terribly nice. I almost wish he would beat me. Because I don't know what to do about the way things are now."

"I think you have to take a little of the blame, too. Surely you could stand up for yourself more."

"No. I couldn't do it when we fell in love. And now, afterward . . ."

"Afterward . . ." said Henrik, in a tone of voice that suddenly made me uncertain. I lowered my eyes and said softly, "Afterward is afterward. There's nothing to be done about it now."

"Be more like Otto," said Henrik vehemently. "That's something you can do. Let me tell you, Otto is someone who knows how to live, that he does. People call it 'living' when a fellow goes off on a spree to find a release for some of the energy he can't use at home doing decent work. But Otto . . . he knows how to work. He's full of vim and vigor. You obviously have no idea what a good businessman he is. He has a *drive* for business, you see, and whatever he gets involved with succeeds, it always does. The trick is that Otto would never set his mind to do anything that couldn't succeed. People can sense that; they trust him. He never, ever wastes his efforts on something. And people always feel that whatever he takes on will be fair. In reality, I'm nothing but a poor devil compared to him—a complete incompetent as a businessman."

"You! If that were true, do you think you would have had such success over in England?"

"Oh, that was mostly luck. By the way, things are more difficult here in Norway; I've noticed that. Out in the world it's easier to hold your own. No, someone like Otto is always moving forward; he lets what's done be done and then seizes hold of the next chapter in life, absolutely convinced that it will be even better. People like him are right—not those of us who sit at the side of the road, pondering about what has happened, dreaming about how it would be to achieve what we *know* it's impossible to achieve."

"People like you and me," I said.

"Yes, like you and me."

"Henrik," I said, "you should see about settling down."

"Oh? And just what do you mean by that?"

"Well, for example . . . you could get married."

Henrik laughed softly. "And that's actually something *you* of all people would recommend?"

"I don't think a man is ever truly unhappy in a marriage," I hastily replied, "as long as he doesn't have a bad wife, that is. For instance, I don't think a man suffers if he marries one person but is in love with another—as long as his wife is attractive and nice."

Henrik glanced at me. "That's not something you know anything about."

I was horrified by what I'd just said—or rather by Henrik's interpretation of what I'd said. I hadn't intended to speak of anything that might refer directly to Henrik and me. At the same time I felt a great satisfaction that the words had slipped out, however much against my will.

That feeling grew stronger as Henrik sat and looked at me, forgetting to avert his gaze. We were sitting on the balcony in the twilight.

"You know," Henrik said very quietly, "if I had told you when you got engaged that things would end up like this, you wouldn't have believed me. Occasionally I thought: it won't work, they're too different. But you were so happy back then. You wouldn't have listened to me, and I thought to myself that things might work out fine after all. I also thought it would be wrong to say anything—and it would have been. You *have* been happy, at any rate."

"It might be better if I'd never been happy."

"No," said Henrik. "It would be miserable, my dear, to have to say to yourself: *happiness* is something that I've never known."

I stood and went over to him.

"Poor Henrik," I said, stroking his cheek.

I felt truly sorry for him—and very touched that he was so distressed on my behalf.

Suddenly Henrik grabbed my wrist hard, his hand burning hot. Then he abruptly stood up and muttered something that ended with "good night." He took his hat from the table and fled.

I was still standing there, completely bewildered, gazing after him, when the nursemaid came to tell me that Ingrid was sick and I needed to come in. Ingrid had thrown up; she had a stomachache and was crying. I cleaned her up and changed her bedding and tried to soothe her. She refused to let me go, so I had to hold her and rock her until she fell asleep on my lap.

I was sitting with her on the parlor sofa when I suddenly gave a start. Someone was standing outside the window. I put the sleeping child on the sofa and went out.

It was Otto. My voice shook with fright and an irrational, guilt-ridden confusion.

"But my dear, what in the world . . . why are you standing out here?"

Then Baby Sister woke up and allowed her father to tuck her into bed. After that Otto came back outside to find me. I was still standing in the dark garden.

"What a peculiar idea you had, to stand here, peering in the window," I told him crossly.

Otto laughed and pulled me into a tight embrace.

"Yes, I know. Sometimes such odd ideas occur to me. I was passing the garden gate, and I saw the light in the parlor. Then I happened to think about what it would be like if I were a stranger walking past on such a beautiful summer night and I saw the light coming from a cozy house in a lovely garden. So that's what I pretended, just for fun. I decided to walk through the garden to see what kind of people lived there. I saw all the beautiful flowers in their garden, I noticed the scent of petunias and mignonettes. Then I peeked inside and saw a charming young woman sitting in the parlor with a lovely child on her lap. God help me if I didn't stand there, envying myself."

And Otto laughed his loud, merry, boyish laugh and again pulled me close. I returned his kiss. We gave each other long, warm, tender kisses, and he put his arm around my waist as we walked among the rose beds.

"It's about time we went to bed, sweetheart," whispered

Otto. And arm in arm we walked back. Then, between two kisses, he said:

"It's obvious that Ingrid is too young to go to children's parties."

His criticism felt like a dousing of cold water on top of all the shifting emotions of the day.

Gently I pulled myself free and went inside. When Otto came in, I rejected any further embraces. I had a headache.

"Henrik was here for supper. He had a headache, too. The air was so oppressive. I suppose we're in for a thunderstorm."

Otto agreed quite affably that yes, we were in for a thunderstorm. And he gave me antipyrine tablets and wondered whether he should leave the window open. If we had a thunderstorm he would certainly wake up. I lay in bed with my eyes closed, smiling wanly, and turned my cheek for him to kiss me good night. And so he kissed my cheek, patted my forehead, and told me to get well. Then he stretched out in his own bed, making it creak.

I WAS REMINDED OF THAT SHIRT in the fairy tale when the girl spills tallow on it and then tries to wash it clean. The more she washes and scrubs, the blacker it gets.

No doubt it was partially due to inexperience, because I had absolutely no experience beyond Otto. I had ended up seeing myself with his eyes, and when the relationship between us became mundane and routine, I was convinced that whether I liked it or not, life would never have any purpose for me except through Otto and the children.

Then I discovered that Henrik was in love with me. I was literally struck dumb with surprise. And I saw that for him, I was my own person, not just Mrs. Oulie and the mother of three little Oulies. I began to observe myself. I was aware that I was what is called an attractive young wife. But I don't think I really gave that any further thought— except to acknowledge that the young girl in the photographs on Otto's desk had disappeared like the snow of last year. Nor was I unaware of the ravages that three childbirths had caused to my charms. Now I discovered for the first time when I looked in the mirror, tightly laced up in a new, light-colored summer dress, with my hair curled and pinned up, that I was really and truly both young and beautiful, in spite of my thirty-three years, three children, and a recently filled canine tooth.

It all began with a secret sort of freemasonry between me and Henrik from that evening on—a melancholy, kindly empathy. For my part, the whole episode has never really had anything to do with eroticism or love. Our meetings, our walks together at dusk, the visits I paid him—when I noticed the danger of what was unforgivable starting to settle over us, making the air heavy—and all of Henrik's caresses. I desired none of these things for his sake but for my own. Me, me, me. I wanted to be adored by his eyes and hands and lips. It was not that I had to surrender myself to the one who had become master of my will—rather, *I* was the one who wanted *him,* body and soul.

It was a natural instinct that broke open inside me, raw

and insatiable. And I, the proper little merchant's wife who went around so nice and quiet, tending to my house, became in reality an evil and dangerously noxious creature. It wasn't exactly vanity but something more intense, maybe whatever is the soul of vanity or the vanity of the soul.

I had no thought for anything in the world but myself. My children . . . I felt it was enough if I saw to it that they had food and clothing, and I wasn't beyond shaming myself with my lover two rooms away from where they lay in bed asleep. Henrik was actually the one I thought about the least. In truth, I cared no more for him than for the mirror on my dressing table. I never thought about what torment our relationship must have caused him. Of course he was a much better person than I was, because he truly loved me, and if only I could have left him in peace, the whole affair would never have happened. It's actually quite unreasonable for me to hate him now. And yet . . . a man of thirty-eight is no naive schoolboy, and he should have respected his friend's wife, for the sake of his friend, even if the wife deserved anything but respect.

Otto . . . I dismissed him with that single phrase: lowly crofter. I went to pick him up when he returned from London, practically gloating, without feeling a scrap of guilt or shame.

I DIDN'T GIVE A THOUGHT to Otto's restless, nervous state during those first days after he returned from his annual business trip. One day he said that he was going to move into his smoking room to sleep, "until I recover from this cough. It will just wake you up, and disturb everyone else." "All right," I said. "I'm very sorry about your cough. I think you've had it ever since spring. You really ought to see a doctor."

I AWOKE ONE NIGHT with the feeling that Otto had been in the bedroom. I noticed that the door to his room stood open—he usually closed it so as not to disturb me or the children with his coughing. I turned over to go back to sleep, but as I lay there half-awake, I could hear that he was up and moving in the next room.

Now wide awake and strangely anxious, I sat up in bed. I saw by the light of the night lamp that it was two-thirty in the morning.

After a few minutes I got up and tiptoed to the door. Otto's bed was empty, and he wasn't in the room. I peeked into the parlor. There he stood, fully dressed, by the window in the corner. He must have heard me come in, because he turned around.

At that instant I saw his face.

Darkness and terror suddenly seemed to flow from every corner of our pleasant, peaceful parlor filled with the gentle glow from the gas lamp outside the bay window.

I looked at Otto's face: pale, despairing, contorted. I saw that he had been crying. "He knows." That was the thought that raced through me.

My heart seemed to split apart, and I couldn't feel the floor under my feet. Then my heart began to pound as a clammy sweat poured from my body, and my hands and feet turned deathly cold. We stood there staring at each other.

"I couldn't sleep," said Otto in an oddly husky and halting voice. "It's nothing. Then I got dressed and went for a walk in the garden. Go back to bed, Marta. It's nothing."

He took a few steps forward and then sank onto the sofa, as if he felt faint. His head fell forward, and his arm and hand rested lifelessly on the table.

Frightened and dumbfounded, I went over to him.

"My dear, what is it? Are you ill, Otto?"

Then he put his head down on the table and wept.

For me, it felt as if life itself, the true, vital life, *my* life, were calling to me when I saw my husband weep. I touched his head, his wrist, bent over him and murmured his name. Then he turned around and pulled me down next to him on the sofa, hiding his face in my lap so I could feel his tears and his burning breath against my skin through my nightgown. It was my own self that came back to me then, the part that had merged with this man, and I wept because he wept. The tears poured from the very depths of my being, the way water bursts out across melting snow.

Otto sat up a bit, rested his head against the back of the sofa, and pulled himself together. He cupped my face in his hands and then gently wiped away my tears.

"Poor, poor Marta. How I've frightened you. Hush, hush, no, don't cry."

After he was calmer he said, "I started coughing up blood in London. Just a little. I went to see a doctor at once, of course. 'Acute catarrh,' he said. Good Lord, that's not so serious, I thought. It's just nervousness on my part. I lay in bed and couldn't sleep . . . and then . . ."

We sat for hours in the dimly lit parlor and talked, trying to reassure each other. Worn out, shivering with cold, damp with tears, I sat with him and spoke comforting, encouraging words, while the memory of what the last month had made of me hovered like a monster spying on me. No, don't look over there, I told myself.

I whispered to Otto and patted his hot, ashen face, as if I were trying to flee from myself and go to him. With my weak hands I tried to hold him up and support him every time I noticed his fear take hold.

Then he told me to go back to bed.

"You're sitting here catching cold, you poor thing."

He put his arm around me and pulled me close. Then in the bedroom doorway he stopped, looked around at the three little beds in the glow of the nightlight, and raised his arms slightly.

"Oh, it's the children that I think about—and you, Marta. What's going to happen to all of you?"

I put my arms around his neck and kissed him.

"My dear, dear Otto . . . acute catarrh? The doctors say that most people have had it and didn't even know."

I told him to go back to bed. I arranged his pillows and covers and talked to him.

"But the thing is, Marta, that Mother died from it . . . and Lydia and Magda. I've never given it a thought before. I've always been so strong and healthy. I always thought that if the two of us couldn't marry with good conscience, then who in the world could?"

I went back to bed but had to get up again to see if Otto had fallen asleep, and I tucked him in as if he were a child. It was daylight by the time I fell asleep.

I didn't wake up until eleven o'clock. When I asked about Otto, the maid said that Mr. Oulie had left for his office at the usual time.

May God in heaven spare everyone from such a night as that.

I wrote a few lines to Henrik, telling him that the whole thing was over, that I was in despair and felt ashamed. Nothing more. I didn't write that I hated him, or that I wished him dead. But that is what I wished with all my soul. If he were gone, it would be as if he had never existed. I longed for Otto with every hour that passed, and I was filled with dread. I imagined that he would somehow find out about the affair. I contemplated all the ways he might find out.

The mere thought of Otto made the old tenderness bleed inside me, a tenderness that is completely physical though it's not desire—the urge to touch, stroke, caress his head, his brow, eyes, lips, hands. A maternal tenderness that had now turned strangely fearful and timid.

IN THE PERIOD THAT FOLLOWED, I lived a life that was like balancing my way along a very, very narrow ledge. It was impossible to look in any direction but forward—otherwise I might grow dizzy and plunge over the side. I lived from day to day, so to speak. Each morning, as best I could, I would forcibly stifle any thoughts except those concerning the day's work, gathering all my strength around one goal: to keep my courage up during the day and display a calm face to Otto and the children.

I could tell that I was pregnant, and I'm sure I felt despair, but it wasn't a new kind of despair—it merely seemed as if the ratchet on the torture rack had been tightened.

Worst of all was Otto's concern for the poor little baby to be born. I could see how he suffered at the thought of it . . . even though after that night he never again showed any sign of weakness or ever complained. And he was feeling tolerably well. He was very careful, and all of us showed as much consideration for his illness as we could. But he kept on coughing, although he was no longer spitting up blood.

We rented a cabin at Vettakollen, as usual, and Otto spent only the mornings at his office.

Fortunately I saw little of Henrik. I actually can't comprehend how I could control myself and act so naturally when we were together. But it was easier for me than I had thought possible.

August 20, 1902

Mia Bjerke came to visit this morning. We talked about my taking a teaching position again.

"I must say it's brave of you, Marta," said Mia. "But it can't possibly be necessary—and besides, Otto is doing so well these days."

I suppose it does seem senseless. Otto doesn't like the idea either.

The others probably suspect that I'm just acting eccentric. That's what they always think.

They have always noticed that I don't really feel at ease with them. And yet they have always been so pleasant toward me. Mostly for Otto's sake, of course, but also because they're nice people.

I was invited to visit the Jensens on the island of Snarøen last Sunday. I sat there thinking the whole time how pleasant it all was—with the overstuffed furniture and the urns and palms and pedestals. But that's not what counts in a home. What matters is not the decor, but what the people are like.

If I were truly talented, as I once imagined I was, then I would have understood long ago that *life is just about people.* Fate is nothing more than people's lives becoming intertwined with each other. And I, who ended up living among such wholesome, nice, clever people, which Otto's friends all are, I had figured out how I could fit in with them. I was able to do it without harming my own being. That *is* possible—there's nothing wrong with choosing and culti-vating those parts of yourself that are useful on a daily basis.

But I've been going around without thinking, precisely when I thought I actually was thinking. I've never tried to see these people from the inside. I judged them from the outside, based on what is not their true selves by any means: their manners and tastes and ideas, which they in turn have acquired from the outside. Take Mia, for example . . . she considers beautiful whatever is modern and on display in the elegant shops. I've latched onto that kind of thing about her and decided that the two of us have nothing in com-mon, yet we're both married and have children.

I was deeply ashamed of myself when she came to see me today. For at least two months I've been thinking about go-ing to visit her but kept putting it off. Then here she comes, bringing me raspberry jam, and strawberries and roses to take to Otto.

Poor Mia. Things aren't much fun for her, either, con-sidering the constant troubles with her children. If I were Mia, I wouldn't be the one bringing roses and strawberries to my sick friends. But as we were coming back from Gref-sen and sat down in the tram, she simply said: "Well, you know, Marta, someone has to endure the worst of things in this world."

Oh, life, life, life!

All those wasted and squandered years when I did noth-ing but go around looking inside myself until I ended up alone even though I was surrounded by people. But I paid attention only to what was happenstance about them—not their true selves.

Even if I've been trained to see things they don't see, and if people have filled my brain with things they don't think about—what does that have to do with life? What does it matter if one person has black hair and another brown, one has a straight back and another stoops? Our bodies breathe life in the same fashion; blood runs through our veins, and we require food and drink. Our souls need the same things, suffer the same hunger and thirst, even though they may have been taught to desire nourishment that is slightly different. Surely we have no other soul than the life of our body—it lives within us like the fire in flammable substances.

So many paths have led me astray . . . But now things are going to be different. I don't know what life is, but it is not loneliness.

Just as we are conceived and born from the lives of others, we must sustain our daily lives with what we receive from others. And we must pay for it by giving of ourselves every single day.

Sometimes when I'm sitting with Otto, I have such a desire to slide down next to him, rest my head on his knee, and say . . . I don't know what. Maybe nothing at all.

I can never talk to him about this. That's why I've written it all down. It's the part of myself that I have separated out and now pushed aside. It's of no use to me in the life that I'm going to live.

I've paid more for my experiences than any person can afford, but there's no use in regretting that now.

The day after tomorrow my boys will be home, and the following day I'll start teaching again. There's nothing to do now but to work for my family, nothing more than that, but nothing less, either. And then Otto will be coming home soon. My own, own, own dear husband!

I feel a stabbing pain that will never stop tormenting me every time I see Henrik and every time Otto caresses little Åse. Maybe I'll get used to it, over time. Others have had to do so. The only thing I know is that I *must* be able to create happiness for my family—and then everything will be all right. It *has* to be.

Part II

New Year's Day, 1903

I've been sitting here, paging through what I wrote last summer. Only four months ago, but it feels as if it were at least four years. Back then I was so certain that everything would work out.

In some ways the autumn has flown by faster than any period in my life, from one Sunday to the next, without my being aware of where the days have gone. I thought the school year had just started, and then Halfred said one day, "Mamma, today it's only three weeks until Christmas Eve."

Einar and Halfred were very quiet on Christmas Eve—especially at first. After I lit the candles on the tree, I couldn't help crying. This year there were too few of us to dance around the tree holding hands. I went into the dining room because I didn't want the maid to see me, or the children, either. Poor things, they should be allowed to forget all their sorrows as much as they can. I remember how it was for me when Pappa died. Even though it made me ashamed and upset with myself, I felt almost angry when, after a couple of months had passed, Mamma would still weep or lament. Children should be spared from grief; that's what Otto says, too.

Halfred came over to me and put his arms around my neck and kissed me. He bravely tried to hold back his own tears. After he left, Einar came in.

They had bought so many presents, my boys. Grapes and flowers for Otto; and for me, in addition to the woodwork crafts they had made, they had bought a pair of elegant, lined leather gloves. I thought it was sheer madness for them to spend so much money on me. But Halfred proudly told me how they had been saving money all autumn.

"And then we met Uncle Henrik on the street last Sunday, and he gave each of us two kroner."

I had the greatest urge to put the gloves away, along with my guilty conscience. But for the sake of the boys, I'll have to keep wearing them as long as even a shred of leather remains.

January 3, 1903

Otto doesn't want to come home. Ever since he had that first violent coughing fit and vomited blood, I think he has understood that he will never return home.

It's my misguided idea to start teaching again that is to blame for his decision to stay up there. But now Otto views it as wise foresight on my part. He has convinced himself that neither I nor the doctor ever believed he would get well last summer, and he has given up all hope. I'm at an utter loss. I can't tell him the real reason for going back to work, and my explanations sound so hollow. But I can't give up my job, which I was so lucky to get. It wouldn't do to keep changing my mind like that, and I have to be prepared to support my children.

Someday when it's all over, I'll have to have a talk with Henrik. So far we've been avoiding each other. One day he said—this was before Otto got sick again—"When Otto is well, I'm going to take a position in London."

If only I could stop thinking about such things, about trying to make a living and financial troubles and drudgery and school, and instead just grieve and grieve, clinging to every minute we have together, the two of us who will soon be parted.

I walk around in a perpetual fever and anguish, tormented by every hour that is wasted when I can't be with Otto. And when I'm there, I sit and grieve and suffer, almost too frightened to speak. I take along my sewing and talk about the children and acquaintances and news from town, or I read aloud from stories that he likes to hear, by Jonas Lie or Alexander Kielland or Rudyard Kipling, deathly afraid to touch on the one topic that we are both thinking about. Then I acknowledge that it does no good, no good at all, this miserly clutching at every drop of dwindling vitality—not the least bit of good.

January 8, 1903

We love each other, and we know that we're going to be parted. There's not a scrap of hope left, no mercy for all our despair. And so we say nothing. We don't scream at life's lack of compassion or weep together. Today we talked about the Bjerke christening.

February 3, 1903

I keep wondering and wondering about how I might be able to get Otto home. Surely it should be possible to find a substitute teacher. But he refuses. He says that he's frightened for the children.

He always asks about Ingrid with such concern since she often has an upset stomach. And the day before yesterday, he finally said (and I could see that he had been thinking about this for a long time), "Are you sure that it's not tubercular? I've been so worried. I beg you to have her properly examined."

I spoke to our family doctor as soon as I got home, and yesterday I took Ingrid to a specialist. They say that it has nothing to do with tuberculosis, but now I feel thoroughly frightened.

March 8, 1903

"I wish that I could stay alive at least until spring," Otto said today.

He can hardly speak anymore. He complains about the pain in his throat, and his eyes hurt, too. His face seems to have shrunk so small, and every time he takes a breath, a horrible big hollow appears under his chin.

March 12, 1903

I get annoyed whenever people try to be sympathetic, and annoyed when they don't. The older teachers at school show such concern for me, and I find that vexing. But the new, young women teachers sit in the teachers' room, laughing and carrying on, nearly bursting with inner merriment. They infuriate me. I begrudge them their joy, and I smile bitterly whenever they talk about life's delights and offer them sharp and scornful words of wisdom. Fortunately, my words don't seem to make the slightest impression on them.

How far I've come from all that. In reality, I don't have the least bit of interest in my job, nor does it give me any joy. I work in a purely automatic fashion. An entirely different world preoccupies me now.

March 19, 1903

The pastor has paid a visit to Otto.

After I took off my coat, Otto took my hand and held it tight. He wanted me to sit down on the edge of the bed.

"Pastor Løkke came to see me today, Marta."

I didn't know what to say.

Otto went on: "I sent word for him to come. You see, Marta, I couldn't stand it any longer. I've been struggling with this ever since fall, when I realized that . . . I don't sleep much at night, and when a person lies awake like that . . . Every night I thought to myself: I'll talk to her about it tomorrow. But then when you came and I saw how tired and worn out and nervous you were . . . then I couldn't do it. I thought you had enough to deal with as it was. And I thought to myself: it's because you're frightened, my boy, that you lie here thinking about all these matters.

"Oh, but that's not the only reason, Marta. Because I didn't think about such matters while I was strong and healthy and had plenty of other things to think about— my business and my home, as they say. But when someone lands in this situation, oh, you can be sure that he knows he has a soul!

"No, Marta, a human life is something very different from all other life on earth. Just the fact that I'm lying here and *know* that I'm going to die, and have to think about it for months in advance, fully aware that it *is* going to happen . . . And those who are left behind, what's going to happen to them? Because, you see, it won't do us any good to pretend to hope any longer, will it?"

I knelt beside his bed and wept. And Otto pressed my hand to his poor, sick chest for a moment.

"Maybe you can't understand this . . . but for me, at any rate . . ."

He lay there, his tears preventing him from saying anything more for a while. Then he whispered in a voice that was even hoarser:

"There *has* to be someone who is stronger than us, stronger than human beings."

I couldn't bear to keep quiet any longer. I felt that I had

to help him in some way, and I whispered, "Oh, Otto, I've been thinking the same thing!"

Then he moved the hand he had placed around my waist to my cheek, and he looked into my eyes and gave me a little smile.

I stayed with him for a long time, such a long time that it was quite dark when I left. Fortunately, I had the company of a lady and gentleman down to the tram. Grefsenveien is so eerie in the dark.

Pastor Løkke had given Otto great solace and comfort with his words. He's apparently such a thoroughly nice and kind man. I agreed with everything that Otto said, and I think it did him good.

"No, Marta," he said. "It can't be true. When a person has brought four children into the world, and the one he loves most is going to be left all alone . . . oh, it can't be true that all bonds are severed at death."

I have no energy to write another word tonight. I feel so miserable and tired from thinking about everything.

April 8, 1903

Today Otto talked about our marriage. He has been aware of much more than I thought.

Pastor Løkke came to see him again today, and Otto talked to me about the one thing that now preoccupies him.

"I feel at peace now, Marta. Oh, it's good to find respite in my faith in the One who is strong and merciful. I never thought that I'd be able to say good-bye to life so calmly, especially when I'm so young and will leave such an infinite number of things undone. I love life, and I was such a strong, healthy person. But now I know that I won't lose any of the things I love, that I'll keep holding on to them in a different way—as if close to my heart.

"I'm happy that you believe the same as I do, that you also know that two people cannot be parted for eternity if they truly belong together. I spoke to the pastor about you today. He says that God does not demand that you accept this immediately with patience and without complaint—but solace will come to you.

"And the children . . . I think, Marta, that I'll be able to see them and follow them in spirit even after I'm dead. Maybe even keep watch over them, in some way. I'm sure that God will be a better father to them than I could ever be . . . but maybe I won't be parted from them, either.

"The two of us, when we meet someday . . . then we'll be able to love each other more deeply than here on earth, because there will no longer be any of the trivial things that have sometimes kept us apart.

"You see, I know that you haven't always been completely happy. I noticed it over the past few years. You've always been a restless creature, my dear. I never spoke to you about it; I was rather afraid that I might make matters worse. Oh, but we mostly had good days together, didn't we, Marta?"

I said yes, and then I wept. It's awful how nervous I've

become; I can't hold back my tears whenever Otto talks that way. But fortunately it no longer bothers him as much now that he has found his faith.

"We've truly always *wanted* the best for each other. And Marta, one day we'll understand and see everything—we'll realize that all the things that came between us were just small, insignificant earthly things that forced their way between us from the outside. They were a result of habit and upbringing and the like. How trivial they were. That's what we'll see when *nothing* in one person's life is hidden from the other."

EVEN IF I *COULD* BELIEVE, would it bring me any comfort? "When *nothing* in one person's life is hidden from the other."

If one day we should see each other's naked soul . . . and truly see how infinitely petty those things were that first came between us . . . But I rebelled in the midst of the riches of heaven, because the One who was almighty and all-knowing had allowed so much misery and shame and corruption of the soul and ugliness to appear—seeping in through tiny little cracks into what had begun so gloriously.

Sometimes I long to believe. I wish I could cast off all of this—my sorrow over this meaningless life and the unhappiness that is irreparable. I wish I could believe there is some meaning to all of it, and some salvation. But I can't. A person would have to give up her own common sense in order to believe in a loving God behind it all—as well as her most basic feeling of decency in order to imagine a salvation made possible through remorse.

The pastor talked about the trials that God imposes to force those who are obstinate to yield—what a slave-driver that God is!

Shouldn't a mother believe in eternal life, Otto asks, since she is the one who gives birth to life? "A child is a letter from Our Lord": that's something I once saw in print. A young girl doesn't really know what she's doing when she allows herself to be given away, with a wreath and a veil and a pastor and bells and music and the Devil, to a man who will destroy her. A poor woman goes out to have a little fun, perhaps to get drunk so as to forget how hopelessly she toils all day long. A girl is assaulted one evening on a highway by some unknown brute. Perhaps they will all receive "a letter from Our Lord."

What does Our Lord have to do with my children? What does a child have to do with eternity? How is a child supposed to live a never-ending life when he started as an egg inside me? If my child were to die just after birth, how would we find each other, someday, much later, when life had ended for me, too? Perhaps I would have tried to believe some of this if I had lost a child.

We humans are supposedly created in God's image— the One who rules the infinite world. I try to think about that . . . and end up thinking about my *own* life, with my nearsighted eyes. I think it's childish babble.

April 12, 1903

I stared until I was blind at the fact that Otto didn't understand me. It never occurred to me that I didn't understand him. We've been walking in the dark, yet were so close to each other that if only I had stretched out my hand, I would have found him at my side. Our young love burned out, and I let it be extinguished, never seeing how easily I could have nourished the fire of a love that might have made things bright and warm for both of us, lasting our whole life. And yet I thought I was so clever.

Otto saw that our life had slipped onto the wrong track, and he grieved over it—not as bitterly as I did, since he always had his work, after all, and he never spent much time thinking about himself. But he has grieved over it and longed for a more intimate life together. Exactly how bad things were, he never knew. Duty and fidelity were for him much too obvious a matter, and he would never have dreamed that two people who married for love and had a home and children together could drift so far apart. I always thought that he saw nothing.

But the matter keeps coming up when he talks, though for him it's now just a shadow of things that once existed. He is done with all that. It has been easy for him to turn to faith—this man who is the very epitome of faith.

He asked me whether I would receive the Sacrament at the altar with him.

"Don't do it if it's not something you want to do, Marta."

These matters can't possibly look the same to you, standing in the midst of life, as they do to me. You should understand that you mustn't do it for my sake, but for your own."

I'm glad that I said yes at once, because I saw how happy it made him.

Now I read the Bible to him every day, and then we always talk about it, although he can't bear to speak very much. His quiet, hoarse whisper eventually vanishes altogether, and I keep having to help him gargle and give him juice to drink. So I read to him.

It's not difficult for me to slip into his way of thinking, and sometimes I feel a certain solace in this pretending to believe. Seen from the inside, there's plenty of consistency in Christianity. It's like standing inside a towering cathedral with stained-glass windows—except that I know that the real world and daylight are outside.

Oh, good Lord, what despair that this is to be how it ends! I tell lie after lie. I don't dare say to him a single word that I truly mean.

Part III

scattered pages

Lillerud, July 1904

What sort of person am I, actually? I thought I was kind and clever. I committed a great sin, but I suppose I believed that it happened without any of the blame being rightfully mine.

Now it looks to me as if I've been more blind and uncomprehending than anyone else. I don't know anybody whose life has fallen apart as drastically as mine has. And surely that has to be the result of some fault inside me.

When I look around the room and see the children as they lie sleeping, I think about what disappointments I'm going to experience through them. Will they, too, slip away from me, like everything else? My life seems nothing but one shattered hope after another, one opportunity for happiness after another that I have refused. Now I'm so tired that I don't really know how I'm going to keep on living. I feel as if I've been crushed inside by a series of falls, and I don't have the energy to get up.

I took out paper and writing materials to reply to Henrik's letter. Whenever I read it, I imagine that I notice a little of the old warmth in him. But I have nothing to say in return. Yet I'm not completely indifferent; I'm glad to know that he still cares about me. I don't think we'll see each other again in this world, but it's rather comforting to know that he's sitting over there in Newcastle still harboring good thoughts toward me. And I think he'll always have them. Henrik is basically a loyal person.

People are complaining up here about the sun, which burns and blazes day in and day out.

I usually sit next to the split-rail fence at the edge of the woods or down near the river. Otherwise, everything is disgustingly scorched here, but the bog is still fresh and green, and the alder shrubs have thick, dark foliage. There's only a little water in the river, but it feels good to sit and listen to the stream murmuring over the rocks and to see the sunshine glinting between the shadows of the leaves, making the water glitter and the insects turn into hovering sparks every time they flit into the light.

Sometimes I walk up to the heights. There's nothing to see but the spruce forest—the uniform, sun-gilded darkness of the spruce forest covering the low, rounded hilltops and, off in the distance against the sun-bright sky, a glimpse of a blue ridge. The peace in the forest on those burning, bright days is as deep as eternal sleep. You can actually sense how faintly and gently the life forces are seeping through the trees and heather. Finally it seems that life has started to move just as sleepily and quietly through my own body and soul, and my sorrow sinks down inside me and falls asleep.

I hardly see the children all day long. They're off at the cabin, playing with the new owner's children. At first Einar didn't want to go over there, but now he has joined the others.

Only Åse putters around the courtyard here with Ragna's little bare-bottomed Tomas. When I take her onto my lap and she sits there chattering, mostly to herself, I both listen and don't listen . . . then I think how inside this small head pressed against my breast there's a whole world. How much of it will I ever know? It does no good to imagine anything else—the souls of my own children are like foreign countries, with an infinite number of long roads that I will never travel. A mother thinks that she knows her children and understands them, but every single child realizes one day that she does not. Yet when I sit with my arms around Åse, I'm not completely alone. With a child on your lap, you're as close to another person as you'll ever be.

FOR THE SAKE OF MY CHILDREN I said yes when Henrik asked me to marry him. I was so tired when Otto died, so tired that I collapsed at the thought of having to make my way alone through the world with the children.

When Henrik sat beside me in the chapel his face was almost as pale as Otto's was in his coffin. And he shivered, as if he were freezing, as Pastor Løkke talked about God's mercy, which had manifested itself in the midst of illness and death, and about Otto, who had wandered the earth, tending to his business and his home with his eyes on the ground, but in those difficult and lonely hours he had turned his gaze upward. Sometimes I recognized Otto's own words, but eerily foreign and distorted, like memories that appear in dreams. Then the pastor talked about the faithful, self-sacrificing wife of the deceased and about his friend and partner.

The whole time I felt that I was dreaming, with the hymns and all the wreaths, the strangers in the procession, all those ominous black top hats crowded together, and many friends I hadn't seen or thought about for years.

It's all been oddly unreal since that morning when I received word that I should come at once.

Otto was conscious and recognized me, but he could barely talk. He had fits of restlessness, and in between he would lie utterly still. Death was completely different from what I had imagined. There would be no real death struggle, the doctor said. But the room was filled with a seething agitation, and Otto, who was holding my hand, suddenly seemed to look away from all of us, stared straight ahead, and whispered, "Jesus . . ."

Just before that, he signaled that he wanted to say something to me, and when I leaned down, he whispered, "You mustn't stand there, Marta—you should sit down, dear."

I COMPLAINED TO HENRIK: "Isn't this a terrible punishment that's been meted out to the two of us? We have to stand here at Otto's grave and think about what we've done, and there's nothing we can do to make things right. We can only regret and regret, and it's completely useless and doesn't do a single living person any good."

"You're right," said Henrik.

"For as long as we live, we'll have to carry this burden around with us. What a misfortune—it dwells inside us like a disease that will never change. And we know that."

"Know? Oh, what do we *know*, Marta? That we're suffering, and that we have suffered? And that we're going to keep suffering? But where does that lead us? We don't have the slightest idea what life might make of our sorrows."

"You may say that. But I know. You speak of life—I'm telling you that life is over for me now."

Henrik did not reply. He merely sat there, staring straight ahead.

"Listen here, Marta," he said at last. "We both are aware, of course, that when a suitable time has passed, we're going to get married."

I leaped to my feet. I was furious. I groaned and raged and showered him with reproaches.

"You betrayed your best friend," I said scornfully. "Seduced his wife. And before he's even been a week in the grave, you come here and talk about our getting married!"

"Yes," said Henrik quietly. "Because that's the way it is. You're right when you say that a terrible punishment has befallen us. But we threw ourselves into the current, and we've washed up where we now stand. Shame and remorse and disgrace—we can't escape them. But we're still alive, and we can't just lie down and die. You have your children.

And I . . . would it help you any if I were dead? Then you would have no one. We've been thrown together, so we had better look at the situation realistically. We will wake up every morning to life and another day that we have to get through—shouldn't we try to live it as best we can?"

"How nice that you can already see it all so sensibly," I said bitterly.

"I think the best thing we can do is to be completely honest with each other and ourselves," said Henrik. "You and I are the only ones who know what we have done. And we've certainly had enough time to figure out for ourselves what it was all about. And also what would come of it. If Otto had regained his health, I would have gone my own way, and you would have had to find some means to make amends with him. But now he's no longer here. The two of us can do him neither harm nor good. He exists only in memory, yours and mine. If we pretend to take him into consideration, it's only ourselves, our moods that we're indulging. Now it's just you and me, and we must try to get what we can out of life. We could wait a 'suitable' period, pretending we were so devastated that we had no thought for anything but our grief. But that's precisely what's so terrible, that we can't grieve without mixing up our sorrow with memories of the past and thoughts of the future.

"Good Lord, Marta, don't you see that sometimes it almost drives me mad, the fact that I can't stand beside you as your brother and your friend and grieve with an honest heart over Otto? Wishing that everything that now consumes our thoughts had never happened, was something we had never known? That if we heard about such a relationship, it would seem to us an aberration that we couldn't possibly understand?

"But it did happen. Why should we play games with each other? Let's at least be honest!"

"Yes. Of course, you're right. But I just don't have the strength to think everything through at the moment. No, I can't see things the same way you do. Oh, Henrik, my life has been so horrible ever since. You have no idea . . ."

"Yes, I do, Marta," he said very softly. "What do you think *my* life has been like these past few years?"

I paced back and forth in the room, crying and moaning. And then I stopped in front of him.

"It's *over*. All of it. Why should we try to build anything back up? What good will it do? And what was the reason that we destroyed each other? A whim, an impulse, that's all, nothing more!"

"Marta, what you call nothing has been my whole life, practically as far back as I can remember."

I stood still.

"You know very well," said Henrik, "that I've loved you ever since I was a boy."

EVEN SO, I DID CONSIDER MARRYING HIM. I hadn't actually said that I would, and we never specifically discussed it, but that was always the assumption.

Henrik came to see me almost daily. He was nice to the

children in his quiet way—took the boys skiing on Sundays and sent them to the theater and such. And toward me he was inexpressibly inventive and patient, trying to entice me out of my stony grief.

Whenever he came to visit, I would sit motionless, the very image of despair, with my eyes cast down. I would actually try to encourage all the torment and weariness and sorrow that had otherwise subsided a bit during the day's work. I would picture to myself how hopeless and unhappy and humiliating the whole situation was—and then I would let him do his utmost to thaw my frozen, mute soul. I let him talk, and I listened with a sorrowfully scornful smile and gave terse, oracle-like replies. But I regarded these visits from Henrik as his duty, and I considered it my sacred right to torment him.

Yes, I tormented him as best I could, and Henrik put up with my moods with the patience and meekness of an angel. I felt no love for him but accepted his love, tugging and tearing at his heart as best I could.

"I have no desire to do anything," I said one day. "There's nothing in life that has any value for me anymore, because I feel as if I've been dragged down into the muck, and I can't get out of it. I'm telling you, I don't even feel like pulling myself up anymore."

When Henrik tried to take my hands, I furiously yanked them away. "Leave me alone!"

"That's exactly what I'm not going to do. You have to pull yourself together. Of course, it's easier to sit down and do nothing but stare into the past, but that's utter suicide. You have to go on. In God's name, let the dead stay buried, and take a look at what you need to do to keep on living—no matter how difficult it may be.

"What good do you think it would do if I sat down next to you to grieve? What do you think my life would be like then?

"I am by nature an honorable man. If someone had told me ten or twelve years ago that one day I would stand here, having done such and such . . . Don't you think I would have sworn it was impossible? I have become quite an impoverished man, Marta. But what's past is past, while the fact that I love you is *now*—and that is what I wish to build my life on."

I wanted Henrik to say things like that. I wanted to see him pour out his love, see him dredge his very depths to find renewed courage to go on living, spill it all at my feet . . . until my incessant grief infected him and I could see and hear that he, too, was dispirited and despairing, and did not believe his own words.

And then at last he would leave, worn out, and I refused to give up until I had driven the life out of his love and stamped out every spark of courage and hope that he possessed.

YET HE KEPT COMING TO SEE ME. He even wanted us to get married. But now it was probably only because he thought it was his duty, so that he could offer as much as possible to me and the children.

As I watched Henrik's love wither, I grew more and more unhappy. It wasn't because I loved Henrik, but I realized that I was driving away the only person who cared about me. And I could see that I had done nothing but work to make him unhappy, and that once again I had understood nothing.

But I still couldn't imagine breaking things off. I felt so ill-prepared to make my own way in the world with the children. To toil alone, year in and year out. I did not even dare think about that.

For the sake of the children I at last put an end to it. If I imagined the future—year after year going from the drudgery at school to the drudgery at home—I was filled with dread. If I thought about how it would be to live with Henrik, in the home we would share with Otto's and my children, and about how I would have to lie and conceal all manner of things from them, then I didn't dare do that either.

On that day in March when I plodded around Frogner Pond for such a long time, thinking until it seemed there was only one choice I could make to be able to live with myself and retain the slightest scrap of self-respect, I felt a kind of release. "After you've done that, you'll have peace," I thought. "You'll see—things will be better."

I don't regret it. It's one of the few things in my life that I don't regret. But neither did it give me any joy. I feel just as much dread for the future. Things have not gotten any better.

I went to see Henrik. As I sat on the sofa near the balcony door and talked, and I looked at his pale, sad face in the twilight, I grew more and more unhappy. I don't know what I said. I think I tried to explain what I'd been feeling all this time.

"It's best if we break things off completely, Henrik. It won't work for us to try to start life over together. We'll just end up hurting each other."

"Oh, no, no, no, Marta. Don't say that—that's not something you can know."

"It's all we've done until now," I said.

Then Henrik grew still. "Nothing but hurt? Is that what you mean, Marta? Yes, I suppose you're right. And yet . . . nothing but hurt?"

"Not you," I swiftly replied. "But I've done nothing but cause harm. And now you don't even love me anymore."

"Yes, I do, Marta. Yet you may be partly right—lately I've thought sometimes that I might not love you anymore. But I was just tired. Now, when you come here and talk like this, I realize that I do love you. My dear, sweet . . . what would be left of me if I didn't love you anymore?"

"But Henrik," I said, "you can see how I am. I've always been so horrible to you, tormented you . . . and I don't love you, I don't love anyone anymore."

Henrik buried his face in his hands, moaning softly as I spoke.

"Oh, yes, Marta, oh, yes . . . People may torment each other—but if they love each other . . ."

"Oh, Henrik, Henrik. This has to end! I'm tired, and you're tired . . ."

"No, I'm *not* tired, never, ever, will I be tired because I love you so much . . ."

Suddenly he began showering me with caresses and pleas and threats, and I don't know what else.

Finally I managed to tear myself away. He sat huddled on the sofa, sobbing, and I stood by the piano.

"You mustn't be sad. I don't deserve anyone's love."

"That may well be," he said wearily, "but that doesn't help me any. I can see that my love is no good, since I couldn't make you love me in return. Because you haven't even understood . . . It's no use. I have no right. My love is completely worthless."

"Henrik," I said. "I know I ought to ask you to forgive me—ask you over and over to forgive me."

"Forgive you for what? Because I love you, but you can't make yourself love me? You're not to blame for that."

He turned away so that I wouldn't see him weep. He went with me to the door and held my hands tightly.

"It's best if I leave," I said. "I'm ashamed of myself. I don't deserve to hear a single word of farewell from you. I don't deserve your sorrow that I'm leaving. And I can do nothing to help you. Let me go, Henrik!"

"Yes," he said, letting go of my hands. "I know that you're leaving. I can't hold on to you any longer."

And he released me, he let me go.

NO, I HAVEN'T BECOME ANY HAPPIER now that Henrik and I have parted ways. But I would have been just as unhappy if I had attempted a future with him.

It's not true that the past is merely something that once happened long ago. At any rate, it's not true for me.

That's what I have been trying to do all along—to put my past behind me. Everything that has happened to me I've tried to see as a story that is over and done with.

But when I sit here in the evening and look back, I sometimes think that everything that happened, and all that remains visible to my eyes, is merely the outward effect. The fact that events have frozen in precisely those shapes is unimportant and almost coincidental. But underneath I can glimpse a shadow—something I can't grasp, something I don't even know what to name, a force of some kind.

It's not frozen or dead. And no matter how my life turns out, how quietly it proceeds or what may occur . . . the shadow that I can't name will follow me. It's moving behind me, it's breathing on me . . .

I'm tired of these useless words of mine. I use them to try and stanch the bleeding of my pain.

I remember something that happened at school during my first year as a teacher. One of the children was run down, right outside the school gate. She got shoved into the street and fell, and a beer wagon drove over her hand. She lay on the sofa in the teachers' room while we waited for the doctor, and we struggled to bind the wound. The blood kept pouring out through all the towels we had wrapped around her hand. The whole time the poor girl flailed her other hand around, trying to tear off the bindings, as she kept screaming:

"I want to see my hand . . . I want to see how it looks."

SIGRID UNDSET (1882–1949) was a prolific writer and one of Norway's most beloved authors. She was awarded the Nobel Prize in Literature in 1928, primarily for her epic medieval novels *Kristin Lavransdatter* and *Olav Audunssøn* (*The Master of Hestviken* in English). Her early novels and stories, often depicting educated but poor working women in the city, introduced a new style of realistic writing to Norwegian literature.

TIINA NUNNALLY has translated more than fifty works of fiction from Danish, Norwegian, and Swedish. Her translation of *Kristin Lavransdatter, Volume III: The Cross,* by Sigrid Undset, won the PEN/Book-of-the-Month Club Translation Prize. She has been appointed Knight of the Royal Norwegian Order of Merit and has been acknowledged by the Swedish Academy for her efforts on behalf of Scandinavian literature in the United States.

JANE SMILEY is the author of numerous novels, including *A Thousand Acres* and *The Greenlanders,* as well as four works of nonfiction. She has received the Pulitzer Prize and the PEN USA Lifetime Achievement Award for Literature, and in 2001 she was inducted into the American Academy of Arts and Letters.